Takeoffs and Landings

Takeoffs and Landings
MARGARET PETERSON HADDIX

SCHOLASTIC INC.
New York Toronto London Auckland Syndney
Mexico City New Delhi Hong Kong Buenos Aires

ISBN 0-439-40665-X

12 11 10 9 8 7 6 5 4 3 2 1   2 3 4 5 6 7/0

Printed in the U.S.A.   37

First Scholastic printing, February 2002

Book design by Paula Winicur

The text for this book is set in Officina.

With thanks to my brother, John Peterson, for his helpful
advice and agricultural information

Lori

Lori stared at her lap. They hadn't even gotten on the plane yet, and already her sundress was a mass of wrinkles.

She'd been warned.

"Oh, that won't travel well," her mom had said when Lori came downstairs for breakfast that morning.

Gram had barely glanced up from flipping pancakes to add, "Why don't you wear one of those outfits your mother bought you?"

That was all Lori needed to hear.

"No," she said. "I want to wear this."

She hated the way she sounded saying that—like she was four, not fourteen. Gram only made it worse.

"She's so proud of making that dress in 4-H last year. Won an Outstanding of the Day ribbon, you know?" she said to Mom, as if Lori weren't right there listening—and perfectly able to speak for herself.

Lori wasn't proud of the dress. She knew the right side seam was just the tiniest bit wobbly, and the facing in the bodice never had lain right, no matter how many times Lori smashed it down with the iron. Plus, she was totally sick of the red-and-white flowered pattern of the material. She'd spent so much of last June and July cutting it, pinning it, sewing it, ripping out bad stitches in it. . . . Her hands went sweaty just looking at it. But, with both Mom and Gram suggesting she change, she absolutely had to wear the dress.

Now, sitting in a contoured plastic seat at the airport, waiting to fly to Chicago, she wished she'd just put on one of her new outfits to begin with. Even though they came from Mom, those outfits were cool, in style, right. Already, Lori had seen six other girls wearing shirts and shorts just like the ones folded up in her suitcase. (For the record: No one else was wearing a squashed-up, homemade cotton sundress.) Mom had shopped at the Gap, Old Navy, even Abercrombie & Fitch. Some of Lori's friends would practically kill for the clothes Lori was refusing to wear.

What had she been thinking?

It was too bright in the airport. In the half-light of dawn that morning, as she'd tiptoed down the hall at home to peer in the full-length mirror without waking everyone up, Lori had had everything figured out. Her reflection had been perfect in that mirror. Her light brown hair arced just right, flowing to her shoulders. Her

2

gray eyes sparkled. None of her stress-zits showed. Half in shadow, the dress was beautiful, perfectly fitted, maybe even the tiniest bit sultry. She'd watched a little fantasy in her mind: *Lori walks into the airport with an air of confidence, striding as casually as if she'd been flying all her life. The crowd parts to make way for her. Everyone is in awe of her beauty, her style, her* je ne sais quoi. *Then someone steps forward. It is an incredibly handsome man—TV-star handsome, movie-star handsome, better looking than any guy in all of Pickford County. His fingers brush Lori's arm, and the mere touch sends a thrill through her body.* (Did that ever really happen outside of romance novels? Lori decided it could.)

"Excuse me," he whispers. *"I am a fashion designer. I must know—where did you get that incredible creation?"*

"This old dress?" In her fantasies, Lori is humble as well as gorgeous. *"I made it. It's a Butterick pattern."*

"Oh, but you have transformed it," the man says. *"You have genius as well as beauty. Will you—"*

And then Lori was stuck. Did she really want this fantasy man admiring her sewing skills? She didn't even like to sew that much. And what was he going to offer her? A job? Not very romantic. A date? Come on, how old would this fantasy man have to be to be a successful fashion designer? She was only fourteen. It was kind of gross if he was too much older than that.

This was a problem Lori often had with fantasies. After a certain point, they just weren't very practical.

Lori might have changed her clothes right then, before she went downstairs. But there was already another fantasy playing in her head: *Lori walks into the kitchen. Mom takes one look at her and stops short.*

"You are not wearing that," she says. "Go change."

"What's wrong?" Lori taunts her. "Are you ashamed of me? Scared someone will find out you've kept your kids locked up in dinky old Pickford County while you're out traveling the world?"

Maybe Lori really would have had the nerve to say something like that, if Mom had out-and-out ordered her to change.

Maybe not.

Lori and her mother didn't really talk. Oh, they spoke in each other's presence—"Please pass the orange juice," "Can I see your report card?" "Do you want me to do the dishes?"—but it had been years, probably, since they'd exchanged any words that actually meant anything. Mom was never around long enough for Lori to move from "Please pass the orange juice" to anything she really wanted to say.

Lori toyed with one more fantasy. She could imagine having a different kind of mother, the kind Lori could sit and talk with for hours. The kind who could help Lori figure out what was going on inside her own head. Lori could imagine telling this perfect mother, *You know what? I think maybe Gram was right. I did wear this dress because I was proud of it. I wanted people to see I was the kind of person who could make her own clothes if she had to. Like I'm as good as anybody out there, outside Pickford County. No—like I'm better. How could I have been so stupid? Why didn't anyone tell me how awful I looked?*

Lori couldn't imagine saying that to her own mother in a million years. The kind of mother she could say that to wouldn't be taking her to Chicago right now.

That would be fine with Lori. She hadn't asked for this trip.

And the longer she sat in this strange, impersonal airport, the less she wanted to go. She felt uglier by the minute. She squirmed in her seat, embarrassed beyond words to be wearing such a horrible, homemade, crumpled sundress. Her hair had gone limp now, too, and her zits were probably as bright as neon signs. If anyone like that fashion designer she'd imagined was strolling through the airport right now, he'd run from her in horror. Probably all the other passengers were staring at her when she wasn't looking and laughing at her from behind their *USA Todays* and their John Grishams. *Get a load of that girl over there. Ever seen such a hick?*

Lori glanced around quickly, ready to glare at anyone hiding giggles. But the only person she caught looking in her direction was her brother Chuck.

Chuck was someone else Lori couldn't talk to. She'd practically forgotten he was there, practically forgotten he was going to be on this trip with her and Mom, too.

Chuck was easy to forget. He was big and fat and

dumb. And that was what people said about him when they were trying to be kind.

Chuck looked away as soon as Lori's eyes met his. Ordinarily, that would have been fine with Lori. But she was so miserable today that his glance away made her feel rejected. Even fat, gross, sweating—ugh—Chuck couldn't stand to look at her. Lori bit her lip, holding back tears. Aside from Mom, who didn't really count, Chuck was the only person she knew in this whole crowded, overly bright airport. Part of her wanted to cling to Chuck, the way she'd clung to him all those years ago at Daddy's funeral.

Part of her wanted to slide down a few seats, so nobody would think they were together.

Mom came back from the bank of phones at the other end of the waiting area.

"Well, that's confirmed," she said. "One of the organizers will meet us at the airport, so we won't have to take the hotel shuttle."

They'd been away from home for only two hours, and already Mom sounded different. Her voice was crisper, more businesslike. She didn't seem like the same person who'd been reading bedtime stories last night to Lori's little sister, Emma, in a lulling, singsongy tone.

No wonder Lori could never talk to Mom at home. Mom-at-home was just a fake, some role she played while she waited for her next flight out.

"Excited?" Mom said, sitting down beside Lori. "Just think—your first plane trip."

Lori shrugged. If Mom couldn't see how far away Lori was from excitement, there was no way Lori could tell her.

Behind her, Chuck only grunted.

Good for Chuck, Lori thought, as if they'd chosen sides and Chuck were on her team. She wished he were. She wished he were someone she could talk to, confide in. She wanted to ask him: *Why is Mom* really *taking us on this trip?* It made no sense. She wished Chuck could explain it to her. After years of traveling on business, why had Mom suddenly decided to take Lori and Chuck with her?

But Chuck wasn't the type of person who had any answers. And it had been years and years and years since they'd been Chuck-and-Lori, inseparable pals. "Joined at the hip," Gram used to joke. Not anymore.

Around them, people were talking in little clusters. Two businessmen types were comparing golf scores. A family with a toddler laughed as the child careened from seat to seat: "Now, come back here and give Grandma a good-bye kiss," the mother implored.

Lori felt like she and Chuck and Mom were an island of silence in the midst of all that chatter. She wished suddenly that the rest of her siblings had come, too—eight-year-old Emma, ten-year-old Joey, and eleven-year-old Mike. Joey would be rattling off a list of questions: *How fast can our airplane fly? What will the ground look like from up there? How high will we be? How many people will be on the airplane?* Mike would be pretending he knew all the answers: *It's thousands of miles an hour, right, Mom? And we'll definitely be above the clouds. Definitely.* And Emma would have Mom's full attention, as usual: *Do you remember when you told me that the clouds look like cotton balls up there? In the Raggedy Ann books, the clouds are bouncy, and you can jump from cloud to cloud. Could someone really do that?*

Most of the time, Lori's younger brothers and sister drove her crazy. But if they'd come, they'd hide the fact that Chuck and Lori and Mom had nothing to say to one another.

Only, Mom hadn't invited them.

Chuck

Chuck was sweating. The backs of his legs stuck to the plastic airport chair.

I'm going to die. I'm going to die. I'm going to die.

Planes went up. Planes went down. Planes crashed. Happened all the time.

He closed his eyes and saw plane parts strewn across a mountainside. Bodies bobbing in the Atlantic Ocean. That one crash had had a lot of kids. A whole high school French club thought they were going to Paris.

Chuck made himself breathe slower.

Mom flies a lot. Hasn't killed her yet.

Yet. She'd never had Chuck along. Bad-luck Chuck.

Lori was staring at him. Why? Oh. He must have snorted. Kids at school always made fun of him for that.

Sorry, Princess Lori, he thought. *Sorry I bothered you.*

You'd think she'd be nicer to him. Seeing as how they were all going to die.

No, Lori would live. She has good luck.

The sun always shone on Lori. She walked on a path of light.

Chuck crawled in darkness, groping his way through the muck.

He saw a face in his mind. Girl from school, wide-spaced eyes, freckles across the nose. A new kid. She was asking somebody: "That's Lori Lawson's brother?"

The girl's eyes bulged, her jaw practically scraped the floor. Like he was Frankenstein and Lori was Miss America. Like Lori was Einstein and he was the idiot drooling in the back of the classroom. Like he was pond scum and she was the peak of evolution.

Well, all that was just about true.

The only thing Chuck had on Lori was being born first.

Far as he could tell, the extra year hadn't helped him any.

Mom was talking now. Chuck focused too late to catch any of her words, but she pointed; he understood. It was almost time to get on the plane.

Chuck's stomach lurched. He pictured his plate at breakfast: five of Gram's thick pancakes, stacked. And then—gone. The plate was empty when he put it on the counter.

Stupid. Shouldn't have eaten so much.

Or not. Why die on an empty stomach?

Did Daddy—?

Chuck didn't let himself think about that. He stared out across the waiting room chairs, all welded together in rows, like a grid. A pattern. People and luggage jammed in the seats and aisles, messing up the pattern. Random. Everyone about to fly. To die?

You wanted this, Chuck accused himself. *You wanted it bad.*

He could see himself, last spring, begging Pop. "Please. I'll do night work all by myself for a month. Just let me go with Mom. I'll pay attention to everything you say. I'll work hard."

Pop chuckling, rubbing his bald head. A little grim. "You should be paying attention anyway. You should work hard all the time."

Pop was right. Chuck was just thinking of the trip as a chance to avoid replanting beans, baling hay, feeding hogs, spreading manure.

No. He'd wanted the trip for more than that. He remembered what he'd thought: *In Chicago and Los Angeles and wherever else Mom wants to go, nobody will know I'm just fat, dumb Chuck Lawson. Maybe . . .*

It wasn't worth hoping for.

He'd always be fat.

He'd always be dumb.

And if nobody else noticed, Lori would always be there, remembering.

Still . . .

All spring, he'd silently cheered Mom on as she

argued with Pop that, yes, Chuck could take two weeks off from farmwork without causing them to slide into bankruptcy once and for all. Even when he didn't like the way she argued.

"You've said yourself he's not that much help, anyway," she'd said one night after Chuck was supposed to be upstairs in his room, doing his homework. "Didn't you say last year that he cost you hundreds of dollars, running over three rows of beans by mistake? I'll be saving you money, taking him away!"

Chuck was in the kitchen, eating peanut butter straight from the jar. Mom and Pop and Gram were in the front room, talking over the noise of the TV. Chuck flattened himself against the wall (as much as he could; he didn't have the kind of body that flattened). He couldn't quite hear Pop's answer, but Mom's reply came through loud and clear.

"Yes, of course I'm joking. I know you're not getting any younger, and you rely on the boys for help. But we're just talking about two weeks here. I'll pay for you to hire somebody to take Chuck's place. I just think it's time for Chuck and Lori both to see more of the world than Pickford County. And to see what I do."

Pop's answer was a mumble again. It might even have been Gram who spoke.

"I'm not saying there's anything wrong with Pickford County," Mom said.

Chuck reminded himself that Gram and Pop were

Mom's parents. They were mostly raising her kids for her. She couldn't afford to cross them.

Hopelessly, he slunk up the stairs, back to the homework he didn't understand.

But the next morning, before taking off on another trip, Mom told Chuck and Lori not to make any plans for the last two weeks of June.

"You're coming with me," she'd said with a broad grin.

Chuck saw Gram nod silently behind her. Pop already had his back turned, as he pulled on his work boots to head out the door.

"I can't go," Lori said. "Jackie Stires always has a pool party the last Saturday in June, and we need to do the Pickford High float for the Fourth of July parade, and then there's my 4-H projects—"

"You can miss a party for once in your life," Gram said firmly. "The float'll be there when you get back."

"And you never start your 4-H projects until July anyhow," Mike chimed in, sneaking in under Gram's arm to snatch a biscuit from the plate she was carrying to the table.

"I do so!" Lori said. "And what about the 4-H pigs? I'm the only one who remembers to feed and water them—they'll never make weight if I'm not around. They might even die."

"It'd be good for the younger kids to take on some responsibility," Mom said calmly. "And Pop wouldn't let them die."

"But why can't we go, too?" Mike complained. Pretty soon Joey and Emma were whining the same thing.

Chuck stopped paying attention.

I'm going away, he whispered to himself.

The crackle of a loudspeaker brought him back to the present.

"We are now boarding rows twenty-two and higher," a woman's voice announced.

Chuck's armpits were drenched now. His hair was plastered to his head with panicky sweat.

"Is that us?" he asked.

Mom nodded.

"No point in rushing to the gate," she said. "We'll wait until the line's down a little."

She sounded so sure of herself, one of the other passengers sat down.

Chuck gnawed his left thumbnail.

It was Gram's fault he was scared.

A few nights ago, when he'd come in late from replanting beans (he hadn't managed to avoid that chore entirely), she'd given him the supper she'd been keeping hot on the stove. Then she hovered over him.

"I never got used to Joanie flying all over the place," she said. "Every time I heard about a plane crash . . . Well, you know. I read someplace that takeoffs and landings are the most dangerous part. That's when planes crash. So I always make sure I say a prayer anytime I know your mom's schedule, the first and the last five

14

minutes of every flight. But now with three of you all flying at once . . ."

She'd bit her lip.

Pop came up behind her and ruffled her hair, like she was just as young as Emma.

"Now, Ida, you know Joanie says those planes are always delayed. Probably sometimes when you're praying that she'll have a safe landing, she's just in the middle of taking off. Don't you worry about confusing God?"

"God doesn't get confused," Gram said stiffly. "And you know you worry, too, Fred. You can't say you don't."

"Aw." Pop waved her concerns away. He sat down beside Chuck and began eating the beef stew Gram slid in front of him. "Haven't you seen those statistics about how flying's safer than driving? The way this kid gets to daydreaming, he's probably safer on an airplane than driving a tractor."

He punched Chuck in the arm, to let him know he was just joking, but Chuck still wanted to protest: *I didn't make a single mistake planting this year. Can't you ever forget anything? Next thing you know, you'll be blaming me again for letting the cows out back when I was six.*

But Pop's expression softened.

"Won't be the same baling next week without having to restack half your loads."

That was the closest Pop ever got to mushy and sentimental. Flying really must be dangerous.

"Chuck? Chuck?" Mom was saying. "Let's go."

Lori was already standing—and making a face that very clearly said, *Come on, stupid.* Chuck scrambled to his feet. Mom picked up the small bag she was going to carry on to the plane. Chuck wondered if he should offer to carry it for her—be manly and all that. But she looked so right with the strap slung over her shoulder, bag balanced against her hip. Someone could take a picture of her and frame it. They could title it WOMAN ON THE GO.

Some magazine had done an article about Mom a year or so ago. There'd been lots of pictures with captions like that, making her sound like Superwoman. MOTHER OF FIVE FLIES HIGH IN "ACCIDENTAL" CAREER, was the headline.

He could almost remember feeling proud, wanting to go around bragging, *Hey, that's my mom.*

But then some of the kids at school had seen the article.

"Your mother's a motivational speaker?" Cassandra Dennis had asked. "Why can't she motivate you?"

The whole English class had heard, and laughed.

Now just thinking about that article made his face hot with shame.

Lots of thoughts did that for him.

He stumbled following Mom and Lori toward the lady taking tickets. Horrified at the thought of falling—he pictured a giant tree crashing in a forest, a beached whale flopping on the shore—he stomped squarely on Lori's foot as he tried to regain his balance.

Lori flashed him an outraged, pained look.

"Watch it!" she hissed.

She even had tears in her eyes. So one of Chuck's last acts would be hurting his sister.

Again.

Chuck watched his feet, heading toward the plane. Toward his doom, probably. He had sympathy suddenly for the hogs that tried to run backward down the loading chute when they were being sent off to slaughter. Chuck hated sorting hogs, anyway—Pop always yelling at him, "Don't let that one past you! He's not ready for market!" and Joey and Mike tattling, "Chuck's not helping!" It was a relief, at the end, when the hogs were all headed up the chute onto the truck. But some hog always balked. He'd turn the wrong way and try to run against the pack. The backward hog would squeal, and the others would squeal, and no matter how much Pop and Chuck and Joey and Mike pushed, the dang hog wouldn't turn around.

More than once, Chuck had seen Pop flip a 250-pound hog end over end, just to get him on the truck.

If Chuck were a hog being sent to slaughter, he wouldn't have the nerve to turn around. He wouldn't have the nerve to squeal. He'd go quietly.

Mom handed a packet to the airline attendant beside the door out to the plane.

"There's, um, three of us," she said.

"Family vacation, eh?" the woman said.

"Sort of," Mom said.

The woman ripped out three tickets and handed the packet back to Mom.

"Have fun!" she said cheerily.

Mom led them through a door and down a hallway. Then they were in the plane, and Chuck had another attack of panic. Everything was too flimsy looking—he felt like he could reach over and crumple the tin of the door with his bare hands. He glanced to the left, and shouldn't have, because that was the cockpit, all those important-looking dials and gauges. But they looked fake, like children's toys. He didn't know what he'd expected the inside of an airplane to look like, but it wasn't this. *This* was supposed to fly?

He looked at Mom, walking confidently down the aisle ahead of him. But that was a mistake, too, because she was tiny and fit easily between the rows of seats. She moved like she belonged on a plane—it wasn't too hard to believe she could be lifted off the ground. Chuck felt like Godzilla trampling behind her. He knocked one man's jacket to the floor and accidentally kicked another man's luggage.

"Excuse me. Sorry," he muttered.

"Who wants the window seat?" Mom asked when they reached their row.

Silently, Chuck shook his head. *What? And have to look out?*

"I don't care," Lori said, though she usually had an opinion about everything. "You can have it, Mom."

A woman behind them cleared her throat impatiently.

"No, you take it, Lori," Mom decreed. "So you can see

out during takeoff and landing. Those are the best parts. Then you and Chuck can switch the next time, so he gets a turn."

Chuck had no intention of switching. He wondered if Gram and Pop were right—that being away from Pickford County so much had made Mom lose a lot of common sense. How could takeoffs and landings be the best parts, when those were the times you were most likely to die?

Chuck eased into his seat. The side of his leg hung over onto Mom's seat. She scooted a little closer to Lori. She was just making room for him, but Chuck felt a stab of self-pity. *Here I am, about to die, and my own mother is trying to get away from me.*

Why should she be any different from anyone else?

Lori

Lori decided she was going to read a magazine during both takeoff and landing. That would show Mom: the last thing Lori cared about right now was scenery out some tiny window. She just couldn't face this trip. The world of *Seventeen*, where everyone had good tans and clear skin and perfect clothes, was her only escape.

But somehow, when the engine began to rumble, and the pilot said in his clipped, official-sounding voice, "Cabin crew, prepare for takeoff," she couldn't help sneaking peeks out the window, just to see what was going on. The pilot revved the engine and then floored it, just like Dan Stephens drag racing on Cuthbert Road. Men—they were all the same, right?

But there was something exhilarating about zooming along the runway, faster, faster, faster. . . . Lori felt herself straining forward, wanting to leave the ground behind. Maybe there was something wrong, and they'd never take off. The engine did sound terrible. But then there was a bump, and the concrete of the runway fell away. Lori heard the wheels of the plane being folded up into the plane's belly, beneath them. It made Lori giddy to think of not needing wheels to move fast. *Hey! Look at me! I'm flying!*

In seconds, they were higher than the roof of the airport. Trees, houses, highways—everything receded beneath them. Nothing looked the same from the air. Lori stared at a blue kidney bean-shaped spot on the ground until it was out of sight, and only then did she realize that it had been someone's backyard swimming pool.

"Great, huh?" Mom said beside her.

Lori turned her gaze back to her magazine.

"It's okay."

Mom didn't say anything else, and Lori let herself look out the window again after a few minutes. They were in the clouds now. Lori remembered the question that she'd imagined Emma asking: *Do the clouds really look like cotton balls?* And they did. It was amazing. The clouds looked just like the cotton batting that her great-grandmother rolled out for quilting.

Lori wanted to tell someone about that idea, but if her choices were just Mom and Chuck, she'd take a pass. Mom would say something like, *Didn't I tell you you'd like this?* That would ruin everything.

Lori glanced quickly over at Chuck in his aisle seat.

Maybe he'd tell Mom what she wanted to hear: how incredible this flight was, how wonderful she was to share it with them. But Chuck had his head back and his eyes shut. His face was pale, making the scattering of pimples stand out more than ever. Pathetic.

Nothing new there.

Lori groaned soundlessly. Two weeks of nobody but Mom and Chuck. How would she survive?

Chuck was going to throw up.

He kept his eyes closed—did he honestly believe that what he couldn't see couldn't hurt him? But not being able to see just let him focus more on his stomach. He felt like the five pancakes he'd eaten had expanded, grown arms and legs, declared war on one another. He felt a retch pushing its way up his throat, and he swallowed hard.

Was this how he'd spend his last moments of life? It figured.

They were taking off. He could tell, the way the plane lurched forward. Some force pushed him back against his seat, like on an amusement park ride. He fought back the urge to gag.

Not being able to see was too horrible. He opened his eyes a crack and saw Mom staring at the seat ahead of her, Lori reading a magazine. Like she didn't care. Gram always did say Lori had a cast-iron stomach and nerves of steel.

Chuck had nerves as wobbly as cooked spaghetti. And a stomach as sensitive as—as—

Jell-O, he thought. And then he began retching. As the plane leveled off, meaning maybe they weren't going to die—not this time, anyway—the five pancakes in his stomach began a takeoff of their own.

Lori

Lori couldn't believe it. Right there, two seats away, Chuck was starting to puke. Lori didn't know what to do. And instead of helping at all, Mom was just digging around in a pocket on the seat-back in front of her. No, wait—she was pulling out some bag.

Did people throw up on planes so often that the airlines gave everyone bags, just in case?

That made flying a lot less appealing, in Lori's mind.

Mom hadn't been fast enough. Someone across the aisle had already thrust a bag at Chuck. But Chuck, being Chuck, didn't see it or didn't know what to do with it. Mom had to shake the bag open, put it right under his mouth, tell him it was there.

Lori couldn't watch, she was so grossed out. And embarrassed. And mad. Didn't anyone but her remember? Back when Chuck was little, he got carsick all the time.

What was Mom thinking, taking him on a plane? What was Chuck thinking, agreeing to go?

Chuck, the eternal fountain of vomit, seemed to be done for now. Mom turned toward Lori.

"Are you all right, Lori?" she asked. "You don't feel queasy, do you?"

"I'm fine," Lori replied. She was trying so hard to keep the anger out of her voice that her words came out flat and dull, like she didn't care about anything. She turned a page in her magazine, and the anger hit her again full force. Why didn't Mom remember? Chuck had a delicate stomach; Lori never threw up. *Don't you know us at all?* Lori wanted to scream at her mother. Instead, she found herself saying, "You should have known. Take Chuck up, of course he's going to upchuck."

Lori wanted the words to come out like a joke, laughing everything off: *Ha-ha. Isn't it hilarious being around Mr. Gross?* But the anger had snuck back into Lori's voice. She sounded nasty, nasty, nasty. If Lori had said something like that at home, Gram would have told her off, sent her to her room, given her some extra chore—trimming an entire fencerow, weeding the whole garden.

Mom just looked at Lori. But that look was worse than any punishment Gram ever doled out. That look could have sliced bone. It was like Mom had the same kind of X-ray vision as the superheroes on the TV shows Mike and Joey watched—like she'd seen clear to the ugly depths of Lori's soul and pronounced, *I don't want you as my daughter.*

Chuck

Chuck felt like he was four years old again, getting car-sick just riding into town. The feel of Mom's hand on his back was the same, the sound of her voice was the same: "It's okay, Chuck. You'll be fine."

Chuck could close his eyes and see the weeds by the side of the road back home: Queen Anne's lace and milk-weed, cornflowers and foxtail, dandelions and clover. And a little boy crouched down in those weeds, his mother bent over him, comforting him: "It's okay, Chuck. You'll be fine."

It sounded all backward, but those were some of his happiest memories from childhood, getting carsick. Not the sick part—that wasn't any fun. But afterward, he and Mom would be there in the weeds, not moving, the sky bright blue overhead, the ground solid beneath their feet. And then they'd get back in the car, where Lori and baby Mike waited patiently in their car seats. Lori wasn't even big enough to see over the front seat, where Chuck had to sit. But she'd call out to him in her little-girl voice, "Chuckie okay? Chuckie okay?" So worried. Neither one of them liked having to sit apart.

That was when they were best friends. That was before.

Did Lori remember at all?

Mom still had her hand on Chuck's back, but she was asking Lori, "Are you all right? You don't feel queasy, do you?"

Chuck's ears were still ringing so badly, he couldn't make out Lori's answer, but he could hear the cruelty in her voice. The contempt. That brought him back.

He wasn't four years old anymore. He was fifteen. Carsick four-year-olds were still cute and lovable. Fifteen-year-olds who threw up on planes were disgusting. He deserved whatever Lori had said.

Chuck shook Mom's hand off his back.

"I'll go get cleaned up," he mumbled.

Lori

The man who met them at the airport was black.

Somehow that made it worse, the way they were presenting themselves: Lori, all rumpled in her stupid homemade dress; Chuck, still reeking of vomit, even though he and Mom had all but hosed him off; and Mom—well, even Lori had to admit that Mom still looked pretty good. How could she have stayed clean, sitting right there beside Chuck while he was doing his impression of Linda Blair in *The Exorcist,* spewing every which way? It wasn't fair.

Not that Lori really wanted Mom covered in vomit.

Did she?

Lori couldn't think straight after that look Mom had given her. She still felt as shaky and jolted and scramble-brained as she'd felt the time she'd touched an electric fence on a dare.

And that was a shame, because she really wanted to

think about what it meant that the man who met them at the airport was black.

There weren't any black people in Pickford County.

Or African Americans—some of the more with-it teachers at Pickford High said you were supposed to call them African Americans now.

From the moment the man had come over to greet them, Lori had wanted to assure him, *I'm not prejudiced. Everybody says people in Pickford County are prejudiced, but I'm not. So don't worry.*

Mom was talking to the man as if she hadn't even noticed he was black.

"Yes, I think we should get Chuck some Dramamine for the next flight. Or those pressure bracelets—I've heard those are very effective."

"Good idea!" the man exclaimed. "My wife and I went on a cruise last winter, and it seemed like everyone we met had those bracelets. Now, that's a cure I wish I'd invested in ten years ago."

He was leading them through a maze of people as he talked. Lori almost wished she were young enough to get away with holding someone's hand, so she wouldn't get lost. She caught snatches of other people's conversation—"caught the twelve-thirty flight" . . . "get to Atlanta before my meeting." A woman was making an announcement over the public-address system, and it didn't even sound like she was speaking English. Lori wished Emma were along so she could hold her hand and pretend it was for Emma's sake.

Suddenly the black man stopped. Lori was trailing him so closely, she almost bumped into him.

"Oh, I didn't even think," he said. "I'm sure one of the shops here would carry those bracelets. Do you want to look for them now, before we get your luggage?"

There were shops all around. Just walking from the gate, they'd already passed more stores than were on all of Main Street in downtown Pickford.

"That's all right, John," Mom said. "We can always pick that up later. Our next flight isn't until late tomorrow."

Omigosh. Mom was even on a first-name basis with this black guy.

The black man—John—went on to other topics. He patted Mom's hand.

"I hope we've managed to convey how thrilled we were that you were available to speak at our convention," he said in a hushed voice. "Roger Palfrew heard you in Dallas last March, when you were at the NJR, and he came back and raved. He said there was no way he'd support us hiring anyone else for our June meeting."

"Thanks," Mom said. "I hope he didn't make me sound too wonderful—I'd hate to disappoint you."

"Oh, I'm sure you won't," John said reverently.

Lori watched with narrowed eyes. John was treating Mom like she was a celebrity or something. Famous. Lori felt like saying, *Come off it. She's just my mom.*

Lori had never paid much attention to the groups Mom spoke to, but now she wondered. What was NJR, anyway? And what group was she going to be talking to here in Chicago?

They went down an escalator into a tunnel of sorts. Bizarre, Asian-sounding music was playing and a sculpture of lighted tubes swayed over their heads as they stepped onto what appeared to be another escalator. Only this one stayed flat, carrying them past arcs of changing colors on the walls. Lori turned to Chuck, finally stunned enough that she had to say something to somebody. With Mom and John up there chattering away like lifelong buddies, Chuck was her only choice.

"Is this weird or what?" Lori muttered.

Chuck didn't even respond, just stood there staring with his mouth open. He looked mesmerized. Lori couldn't stand it.

"Catching flies?" she asked. That was one of Pop's expressions. She missed Pop suddenly. He'd be the first to agree with her that this tunnel was weird. He was all the time saying, "Never can tell what some fool will come up with next," while he was watching TV or reading the newspaper. Lori could just picture him, announcing that while he shook the newspaper for emphasis, in disgust. If Pop saw even a picture of this tunnel, he'd laugh his head off.

Chuck mumbled something just then, and Lori leaned in closer to hear him. You couldn't expect words of wisdom from Chuck, but after what she'd said on the airplane, she owed him.

"Huh?" she asked.

"It looks like the future," he repeated.

Weird, Lori thought. *Definitely weird.*

32

Chuck

By the time they got to the hotel, Chuck was in a total daze.

Already, it seemed a million years since he'd made a fool of himself, throwing up on the airplane.

At least the landing had made him only slightly queasy. And he'd been so worried about throwing up again that he'd forgotten to worry about dying.

The plane had dipped to the side a little, landing, and he'd caught a glimpse out the window. An ocean sparkled in the sunlight—no, it wasn't an ocean, just a lake. He knew that much. But he'd never expected a lake to be so big. The downtown was just as amazing—all those enormous buildings. If they looked enormous from the air, what would they look like from the ground?

The sight made him feel big and small, all at once.

Then there was the airport.

He felt funny just thinking about the tunnel they'd walked through, going to get their luggage.

Lori had called it weird.

Maybe he was supposed to think it was weird, too, but he got mad hearing her say that. Didn't she *see*? All those lights and colors, and the music—it was crazy and wonderful all at once. It made him feel like dancing or something, not that he had ever danced.

Were he and Lori looking at the same thing?

He liked all the different people around them, too. The man who met them had skin with the sheen of home-made chocolate pudding. The color was so rich and deep that Chuck had to keep telling himself not to stare. He thought about the box of crayons he'd had when he was a little kid. There'd been sixty-four in the box. Had that chocolate pudding color been in there, too? He couldn't remember.

He didn't know why it mattered so much, a little kid's crayon. But it did.

The taxi driver was black, too, or what people called black, but his skin was a different shade entirely. When he talked, Chuck couldn't understand him at all.

He bet Lori could, though.

"It's the one on the left," the man, John, was saying. "You can pull in at the circular drive."

The taxi driver said something, and Chuck couldn't make sense of a single syllable. But somehow, he knew the taxi driver was complaining. *Don't treat me like an idiot. Don't you think I know what I'm doing? Who gave you the right to boss me around?* Chuck was suddenly filled with deep respect for the taxi driver. If only Chuck could stand up for himself like that. He wished he could repeat the words the taxi driver had said. It'd be nice to toss out some foreign phrase the next time the kids picked on him at school or Pop yelled at him for forgetting to lock the barn.

They stopped and the taxi driver began pulling their luggage out of the trunk. Chuck went over and picked up his own suitcase—still looking as new and unused as the picture in the Penney's catalog Gram had ordered it from. Then he reached for Mom's, which was a little more battered. Seasoned. Mom turned around and saw what he was doing.

"Oh, Chuck, you don't have to worry about those. Leave them for the bellhop."

"Huh?" Chuck said.

"Someone from the hotel will carry our bags for us," Mom explained.

Face flushed with embarrassment, Chuck dropped the bags. Both John and the taxi driver were looking at him. Chuck retreated to the curb, wishing the sidewalk would swallow him up. He could live in the sewers of Chicago for the rest of his life, if only he didn't have to see the look of scorn on Lori's face.

It wasn't fair. If Pop had been along and Chuck had stood aside like Mom said he should, Pop would have yelled at Chuck for being lazy. That was one of Pop's favorite complaints about Chuck; how many times had Chuck heard, "You're not carrying your own weight!" hollered at him across a barn or a hay wagon or a cornfield? The words always seemed doubly cutting, considering that Chuck's weight would be a lot for anyone to carry.

Chuck watched the taxi driver take their suitcases to a man in a uniform, who stacked them on a rolling rack and pushed them through the automatic doors.

It was nice not having to carry his own suitcase. But he could hear Pop's voice growling in his head. *Why should someone else carry your suitcase for you, when you're able-bodied and perfectly capable of doing it yourself?*

Was it Pop's voice or what Chuck thought himself?

Lori leaned toward the huge wall of mirror to apply lip liner. She had to admit, it was a lot easier to see to put on makeup here in the hotel than back home, looking at Pop and Gram's cracked bathroom mirror. The crack went right through the middle of her face, so she either had to stand on Emma's old bathroom stool to see her face whole or duck and weave to look around the crack.

Mike and Joey had broken the mirror a month ago, throwing a football inside the house. Gram and Pop hadn't fixed it yet, as a reminder to them all not to play so rough indoors. Lori didn't think that was fair. *She* hadn't broken the mirror. And it didn't punish Mike and Joey at all, because they didn't even look in the mirror to wipe their faces. Lori thought Gram and Pop were just being lazy. They didn't care about the bathroom mirror because *their* bathroom, the only one *their* company ever saw, was downstairs, newly remodeled.

Mostly, Lori got along with Gram and Pop, so it was weird that she was resenting them now. Usually, she reserved all her ill feelings for Mom. Okay, here it was: Lori thought Mom was the one who'd paid for Gram and Pop's remodeled bathroom. Once again, everything could be traced back to Mom.

Lori stuck her tongue out at the gleaming hotel mirror. *Take that, Mom.*

Then Lori giggled at her own reflection. She felt too good now to get all bent out of shape about a stupid mirror. She had control of herself again. She could handle this trip. She'd even—almost—had fun today.

They'd had lunch in an outdoor café, walked along some river, looked at skyscrapers. They were going to go up inside a building that was or used to be (or something) the tallest in the world. But then Mom got worried that the elevator might upset Chuck's stomach again.

It figured that Chuck would ruin things. But Lori didn't care. The first day of the trip was almost over. She had only thirteen more days, and then she'd be home again planning swim parties with Angie and Dana, discussing boys with Courtney and Bree, going to movies and 4-H meetings and all-county dances.

That was the way to think about this trip.

Mom knocked on the bathroom door.

"I need to be down there in a few minutes. Want me to go ahead? Someone at the door can tell you where to go."

Lori decided her lips looked good enough.

"No, no. I'm ready." All her resolutions aside, something about this glitzy hotel made her want to stick close to Mom and Chuck. It was so big, Lori thought she'd never find herself if she got lost.

She didn't want to have to ask anyone for directions.

Lori came out of the bathroom, then it was Chuck's turn. He didn't have to do anything but wet down his hair (which made it look greasy) and tuck his shirt into his dress pants. It was untucked again in five seconds, because the material had to strain so hard to make it over Chuck's stomach.

Lori looked away, toward Mom.

Even Lori had to admit she looked great.

Mom was the sort of tiny woman who could look like a little girl dressing up in her mother's clothes if she wasn't careful. Lori had said that to her once.

"What am I supposed to do? Draw wrinkles on my face?" Mom had said.

Mom had practically the same pixie haircut as in the first-grade picture of her Gram and Pop still kept hanging in their living room. But tonight she'd used strategic amounts of gel on it. Her dark eyes were highlighted with a precision that Lori's fashion magazines would praise. Her purple suit was classy—not too prim, not too outrageous.

Lori practically approved.

Not that you'd ever catch her saying so.

"Let's go then," Mom said. She looked both kids up and down, then turned on her heel for the door.

You might have told us that we looked good, Lori thought. *Or at least me.* She'd crumpled the homemade sundress into the bottom of her suitcase hours ago (maybe explaining why she'd felt better all afternoon). Now she wore one of those ankle-length floral dresses just about everyone owned. Pure polyester, Gram would have said, but who cared?

Lori followed Mom and Chuck onto a glass elevator overlooking a lobby many floors below. Even through the elevator, they could hear tinkly music being played on the grand piano, right next to an indoor waterfall.

Fancy-schmancy, Pop would call it. In spite of herself, Lori liked it. She remembered a song Pop had sung for her once when she was doing a family history project for school: "How Are They Gonna Keep Them Down on the Farm Once They've Seen Paree?" Pop's own grandfather had sung it to him, because he'd fought in World War I. "Paree" was really Paris, and Pop's grandfather had really gone there during the war, but he'd hated it. "Filthy people, filthy houses, filthy food, and nobody can talk right. Plus, all those so-called French beauties ain't any prettier than spit," had been his report on the city, according to Pop. "Give me the farm any day."

Lori had always been inclined to side with her great-great-grandfather. Chicago wasn't Paris, of course, and it wasn't so bad to visit. Just so you got to go home afterward.

They got to the huge banquet hall, and Mom showed Lori and Chuck their seats.

"I'll have to be up at the speakers' table during the meal, too, but you'll know where to find me if you need me," she said, just like they were Emma's age. Lori rolled her eyes. Mom didn't seem to notice. "I'll come and get you afterward," she finished.

The other people at Chuck and Lori's table were business-people who gave them "What are you doing here?" looks and then ignored them. Lori picked at her dinner: stringy chicken, lumpy rice, and tough pellets of zucchini. Lori tried to imagine what a 4-H cooking judge would have to say about the meal, but that was a boring game. Lori didn't even like 4-H cooking projects. She just took them because everyone else did. You had to win your blue ribbons somehow.

Lori was actually reduced to daydreaming about whether she should take chicken croquettes or chicken divan to the fair for her cooking project this year when she heard an announcer say, "Our speaker for this evening . . ."

Lori turned around and started paying attention.

He seemed to be introducing some other person—some wildly successful businesswoman—but then he said, "Joan Lawson," and Mom stood up to a burst of applause and even a wolf whistle or two. You could tell she was standing on a stool, but the man still had to bend the microphone down for her.

"Thank you," Mom said firmly, making a motion with her hand that effectively ended the clapping. "I knew I could 'count' on a group of bankers for a warm reception."

41

It was an utterly lame joke, but somehow Mom made it sound funny.

"People are always saying time is money," she continued. "I figure that's something you all would know about."

For some reason, getting behind the podium made Mom sound different. Her vowels got longer, and the "you all" practically became one word. She sounded like she was from the Deep South, instead of southern Ohio. What was that all about?

"I just can't see someone walking into your bank, strolling up to one of your tellers, and declaring, 'I've got a little spare time on my hands right now, and I'd like to open an account. What kind of interest are you offering on deposits of three hours or more? Will it be up to four hours by the time I'm fifty-nine and a half?'" Mom was saying. "'How many minutes will I have to forfeit for early withdrawal?'"

Lori didn't get it. Sure, she understood that Mom was pretending that time really was money and that people could put it in the bank like dollars and cents. But why were the people around her practically falling out of their seats with laughter?

Mom went on and on, in that strange, folksy, down-home voice. Then she stopped and looked out at the crowd, waiting for the laughter to die down. When everyone was silent, she shrugged and said, "Now, that's just silly, isn't it?"

The whole room burst into laughter again, as if everyone was just waiting for another chance to be silly together.

These bankers must not get out much, Lori thought.

"But, you know," Mom continued in a more serious tone. Even her drawl flattened out a little. "For all that we keep saying time is money, we all really know it isn't. The problem is, we seem to have forgotten that money isn't time, either."

She paused, letting her words sink in.

"I have five kids. Back when I had three of them in diapers all at the same time—and usually all dirty at the same time, too, I might add—there were some days when I thought I'd need about five more of me just to take care of my own children. Money wasn't in very great supply back then either, so I didn't often have the option of hiring someone else to take care of my kids for me. I'm not holding myself up as some sort of saint here—there were times when I would have paid every penny I had just to have someone else get my daughter Lori ready for church. When she was two, she was an escape artist when it came to clothes. No sooner would I have the last button on her dress buttoned, and turned around to keep the baby from chewing the bow tie off his collar, than I'd turn around again and Lori would have stripped entirely. The dress, her tights, and even that frilly white underwear would be lying in a heap on the floor, and she'd be dancing around naked, ready to run out the door." Mom grinned. "My husband was a little concerned about what sort of career possibilities she was getting inclined toward."

The bankers laughed again, uproariously. The sound swelled in Lori's ears. Her face burned. *This* was what Mom had been talking about, all these years, all across the country? Making fun of Lori? How dare she.

Lori couldn't stand to listen to another word. She got up and rushed for the door. She was glad now that nobody at their table knew who she was.

The tears were already swarming along her eyelids, but she kept her eyes open wide so none of them would start spilling over until she was alone. She hurried across the glitzy lobby she'd been so impressed with before and stabbed the elevator button. Seventeen. They were on floor seventeen. . . . Only sixteen more floors to go.

Fortunately, the elevator was empty, and Lori let herself sniffle as soon as the door closed. Lori felt so ashamed. Had people seen her leaving? Did they know she was Mom's daughter? Did anyone think, *Well, there's the little striptease artist now*?

Probably they laughed even harder, if they knew.

The elevator dinged and the doors opened. Just a right turn and a left turn, and then Lori would be safely back in her room, and she could cry and cry and cry, all she wanted.

Lori was at the door of room 1709 before she remembered: She didn't have a key.

Chuck had never known.

Mom—*his* mother—was incredible. For the first seven years of his life, she'd been just Mom, making meat loaf, checking his homework, reminding him to wear his jacket when it rained. And then, after that, after the accident, when they moved in with Gram and Pop, she was still just Mom when she was around. She just wasn't around as much.

He'd known she gave speeches. He'd known she gave a lot of them. But he hadn't known she was like an actress up there, getting people to laugh just by screwing up her nose and making a face. He hadn't known she could make a whole room quiet just by standing still and waiting. And he hadn't known she was so smart. She was talking about time and money and banks like—well, like she didn't even come from Pickford County.

Chuck was so proud.

He sat tall in his squishy banquet chair. He forgot that the banquet meal had been so small and that he was still hungry. He forgot that neither Lori nor anyone else at their table had spoken to him for the entire meal. He was in awe.

"I have five kids," Mom said, and Chuck felt a little jolt of surprise. It was almost like he'd forgotten she was Mom. But of course she was talking about him and Lori and Joey and Mike and Emma. It was almost like they were famous, too.

Mom told a funny story about Lori when she was two, how she always took her clothes off as soon as Mom got her dressed for church on Sunday mornings. The entire banquet hall was laughing—as Pop would put it, fit to split their pants.

"You had to admire her persistence," Mom said with a shrug and a smile, like she'd been proud of Lori even though she'd been exasperated.

Chuck turned around to whisper to Lori, *She's talking about you!* But Lori wasn't there. Chuck puzzled on that for a minute. Would she really have gotten up to go to the bathroom in the middle of Mom's speech? You never could tell with Lori. Too bad—she missed hearing Mom talk about her. But having Lori away probably saved Chuck from another nasty look. If Chuck had whispered, *She's talking about you!* Lori would have only frowned and rolled her eyes, saying without words, *No, duh! Don't you think I recognize my own name? I'm not that stupid. Not like you.*

It was just that Chuck wanted to share this moment with Lori. He wanted her to agree with him: *You're right. Our Mom is really somebody!*

He turned back around to enjoy the rest of the speech.

WHAT JOAN LAWSON WANTED TO SAY
DURING HER SPEECH IN CHICAGO:

See those two kids out there? That's right, the only two people under twenty in this whole crowd. Those are my kids.

Only, I'm not sure I have the right to call these two "my" kids anymore.

Can someone lose her own children? Not because they died, not because anyone kidnapped them, just . . . because?

I'm afraid that might have happened to me. No, I'm terrified.

You see a pretty, self-assured—maybe too self-assured—girl in a flowered dress and a slightly overweight (okay, very overweight) boy looking down at his plate.

I see echoes, memories, ghosts. Accusations.

With the others—Mike, Joey, Emma—I am still Mom.

Emma begs for bedtime stories; Mike and Joey show off their latest karate moves. They are glad when I come home.

But Lori volunteers to do the dishes when I'm around just so she can hide out in the kitchen and avoid me. Chuck won't look me in the eye.

I thought this trip would change everything. Good old magnanimous Mom, cashing in almost a decade's worth of frequent flier miles for Lori and Chuck. But they don't want what I have to give them.

Poor Chuck retched a few times on the airplane, threw up a teaspoon or two of bile and acted as shamed as a dog beaten for ruining a carpet.

Then he positively cringed when I told him the bellhop would carry his luggage.

What makes Chuck act so guilty? Why does he accept humiliation like it's his natural due?

I don't know how to help Chuck. I seem to only push him further into his shell.

Then there's Lori—I can still hear her cruel words on the plane reverberating in my ears: "Take Chuck up, of course he's going to upchuck." I am her mother. It's my job to tell her not to say things like that, not to hurt people like that. But I could say nothing. I couldn't bear to scold her, push her further away.

I am paralyzed around my own children.

And I am supposed to be standing here telling all of you how to live your lives?

I am more frightened of giving tonight's speech than I

have been of any speech in years. Maybe ever. I am sure that my kids will see through me, will see that I don't have any answers. But I am speaking and words are coming out of my mouth and you all are listening and laughing at the right time, so I must be saying what I'm supposed to say. I just can't read my kids' expressions. I can't see what they're thinking. I can't—

Wait a minute. Where did Lori go?

WHAT JOAN LAWSON ACTUALLY SAID
DURING HER SPEECH IN CHICAGO:

The truth is, we do have our time in a bank. Unlike any of the banks you all operate, though, we aren't ever allowed to know how much we have left in the time bank until we've spent it all. All we can know is that we get to withdraw twenty-four hours every day. Everyone from the top of the Forbes 500 list to the poorest third-world orphan gets the same amount. But what you do with your daily withdrawal of time is entirely up to you. . . .

When the day comes that—surprise!—you find that you have drawn out every last second in your account at the time bank, that is not the moment to suddenly realize, *Oh no! I was going to start my own business!* or *Oh no! I was going to leave the rat race and move to Maine!* or *Oh no! I was going to spend more time with my family!* Say your "Oh no"s right now, while you still have time in your account. Do what you need to now, so you won't have regrets when your account is closed.

Chuck

Mom's speech was over and people were clapping. Chuck closed his eyes for a second, and the pounding applause became a picture in his head—swirls of sound climbing higher and higher, like stairs he could never climb.

When he opened his eyes again, someone else was at the podium, thanking Mom, praising Mom, telling everyone to applaud again. And then Mom was snaking her way through the crowd. Toward him.

She caught his eye and mouthed something, but he didn't understand. People were trying to talk to her, but she shook them off and kept walking.

Why was she in such a hurry to get to *him*?

But as soon as she got close, he understood.

"Where's Lori?" she demanded.

Of course. It wasn't Chuck she wanted. He should have known that.

Chuck glanced over his shoulder. Lori's seat was still empty.

"I don't know. Guess she had to go to the bathroom," he said.

"But she disappeared a half hour ago," Mom snapped. Chuck had never known Mom could sound so much like Lori. "Didn't she tell you where she was going?"

Chuck shrugged.

"Come on!" Mom commanded.

She whirled around. It was all Chuck could do to keep up with her.

Outside the huge meeting room, Mom stopped only to ask someone where the nearest bathroom was. For a minute, Chuck was afraid she expected him to follow her in. But when they got to the door of the ladies' rest room, she gave another command: "Wait here."

Chuck stood on a rosette in the carpet. He could hear Mom calling through the wall, "Lori? Lori? Lori, are you in here?"

In seconds, Mom was out again.

They tried every bathroom on the main floor of the hotel. Then Mom raced to the front desk, dragging Chuck behind her.

"My daughter is missing," she all but barked at the man behind the counter. "She's fourteen. Light brown hair, greenish gray eyes, about five four. She was wearing a blue flowered dress. Ankle length. Have you seen her? Did you see her leave with anybody?"

The man blinked. Mom didn't even wait for him to answer.

"You have security tapes, don't you?" she asked.

"Your security people will need to review them. Please."

"Ma'am, calm down," the man said. "Are you sure you haven't just missed connections with her? That happens all the time—one person thinks everyone's meeting back in the room, the other person thinks they're meeting in the lobby. . . ."

Mom looked quickly at Chuck, then looked away. Chuck understood: Mom had just decided he couldn't be trusted to go check the room by himself.

"My son and I will go look in our room," Mom said. "But in the meantime, could you please contact security? Call me. I'll be in room 1709."

The elevator ride felt endless. Mom kept biting her lip and looking at Chuck nervously. Chuck didn't know what to say. When the elevator reached the seventeenth floor, Mom was out the doors before they were completely open. By the time Chuck caught up with her, she'd already zipped in and out of the room.

"She's not there," Mom said. All the color was gone from her face. "I'm going back downstairs. Call me at the front desk if Lori shows up. And no matter what you do, don't leave."

Mom disappeared down the hall.

Chuck stood at the door, left behind.

He backed up until he was sitting on the bed. He watched the door glide toward the doorframe, and stop. And then, even though nothing moved, nothing changed, he kept watching that door, memorizing every shadow and groove, as if that could help find Lori.

Lori heard the elevator ding. She fought to regain her self-control—all she had to do was keep her sobs silent until whoever was getting on or off the elevator passed by and out of earshot. She'd found the perfect place for crying: a little alcove around the corner from the elevator on the seventeenth floor. She was thoroughly hidden by a huge, fake potted plant. And as long as Lori didn't make any noise, nobody would turn this way, because all the rooms were in the other direction.

Lori had managed to keep quiet through three elevator arrivals and departures already. She was terrified that someone—a kindly bellhop, a curious maid—might discover her and try to comfort her. Lori didn't want to be comforted. She wanted to cry and cry and cry, wail and scream, until she could face Mom and Chuck (and hundreds of bankers?) again.

All she had to do was wait a minute or two, and then she could go back to sobbing. . . .

Lori listened for the elevator to leave. She could feel the wails building inside her. Even though she had her lips clamped tightly together, a moan escaped.

Footsteps came toward her, muffled by the thick carpet.

"Lori? Oh, Lori!"

It was Mom. She held out her arms like she expected Lori to do some Prodigal Son routine, throwing herself at Mom and begging forgiveness.

Except Lori hadn't done anything wrong. Everything was Mom's fault.

Lori didn't budge.

"Where have you been?" Mom asked.

"Here." Lori sniffed. She would have said more, but her throat betrayed her, closing over and choking out all Lori's words. Lori knew just how she looked: red eyed, runny nosed, tear streaked. It wasn't fair. Mom still looked great.

"Why?" Mom asked, looking genuinely bewildered. For a split second, Lori could have run to Mom, cried on her shoulder. Then Mom said, gently, "What happened?"

She honestly didn't know. She didn't understand at all.

"I didn't like your speech," Lori mumbled.

Mom's expression changed in an instant, hardening into fury.

"Fine," she spit out. "You didn't like my speech. That's no reason to scare me to death. Didn't you know how worried I'd be? What did you think I'd think when I finished my speech and you were gone? I'll tell you what I thought. I was imagining you dead in some dark alley or kidnapped or raped or—or . . . This is *Chicago*. It's a big city. You're not in safe little Pickford County anymore—"

Lori couldn't stand it.

"I know," she interrupted. "In Pickford County, mothers don't make fun of their kids in front of thousands of people."

Mom drew back as though Lori had slapped her. Lori was afraid she'd gone too far. Kids in the Lawson family were not allowed to talk to grown-ups like that. And Mom was already mad.

"What do you mean?" Mom said sharply.

"'We were afraid Lori would grow up to be a strip artist—'" Lori quoted.

"That's not what I said!" Mom protested.

"Close enough," Lori hissed. She knew Mom had really said, "My husband was a little concerned . . .," but it was too dangerous to bring up Dad. Just saying his name would be like hauling a nuclear bomb into their battle.

"Lori, that was just a story. You were two years old, for crying out loud."

"Yeah, well, I'm not two anymore. How do you think it made me feel, hearing that? To know that for eight years you've been saying God knows what about me to all these strangers? People I don't even know?" Lori held back a wail. If she was going to fight with Mom, she wasn't going to be all weak and teary. "I mean, you were talking about diapers! How many bankers in America know the intimate details of how I was potty trained?"

"Oh, Lori." Mom slumped against the ritzy, expensive-looking etched wallpaper behind her. Everything around them was too fancy. Lori wished they were fighting someplace real.

But someplace real, Lori wouldn't have the nerve to say anything. Beside fake trees, seventeen stories above ground, Lori couldn't stop herself.

"Maybe you want to be famous and have all these people oohing and aahing over you, but what about me and Chuck and Joey and Mike and Emma? Don't we have any rights to privacy?"

"Oh, Lori," Mom said again, and took a ragged breath. "When I started giving these speeches, I didn't know anything. I was just a high school graduate, and I was talking to people with college degrees—doctorates, some of them. The only subject I was an expert in was you kids. The only thing I'd ever studied was the way you all looked taking your first steps, the smiles you gave out, the—the way you smelled, fresh from your baths—"

Lori couldn't listen.

"Save the flowery descriptions for the bankers," she said, brushing past her mother. She had to get away from Mom. She was terrified of what she might say next if she stayed. "That was all a long, long time ago. Did it ever occur to you that you aren't an expert on any of us anymore?"

She was down the hall now, but she couldn't resist shouting back, "Given how little we've seen you the past eight years, I'm surprised you even remember our names, let alone any cutesy anecdotes about how we looked taking our first steps."

She rounded the corner, wanting mostly to find a door so she could give it a good, satisfying slam. But she'd forgotten: She still didn't have a key to room 1709. She didn't have anywhere else to go, though, so she ran to the room, anyway, and gave the door a hard kick, instead of knocking. It swung open. It must not have been fully latched.

Chuck sat on the bed, blinking at her.

"Um, Mom's looking for you," he said blankly. "I think she's kind of worried."

Lori wanted to be home so she could flounce upstairs and shut the door of her own room so hard that the whole house would shake. She wanted privacy. She wanted to be alone. She settled for going into the bathroom. But the door must have been designed to prevent slamming—even her hardest shove sent it only gliding gently closed.

Somehow that made Lori madder than ever.

Chuck

Mom came in only a few minutes after Lori.

"Lori's here," Chuck said. He inclined his head toward the bathroom door. "In there. I was just going to call the front desk, like you said—"

"I know," Mom said. "I saw her. We talked."

And then she practically dived onto her bed, burying her face in her pillow. She lay without moving.

Things were getting really weird.

Lori

Locked in the bathroom, Lori slumped against the cold porcelain tub on the cold tile floor. She couldn't cry with abandon anymore because Chuck was right there on the other side of the door. She tried to distract herself.

She remembered a story Gram had told her once about Mom.

When Mom was fourteen, she'd started showing off one day in the hog barn at the Pickford County Fair. She'd turned cartwheels the whole way down the barn's aisle, not seeming to care at all that her hands and her sandals might easily end up covered in a stinky mess. She'd landed right at the feet of, as Gram put it, "that good-lucking Lawson boy." And instead of being embarrassed, Mom had raised her arms high, victoriously, like a real gymnast.

The next thing anyone knew, Mom and Dad were going out.

But that wasn't the end of the story. Pop had gotten wind of Mom's feat, and he went around telling all his friends about it at Farm Bureau Council and down at the Pickford Farmers' Exchange. Lori could just hear how he'd say it: *Can you believe my own daughter doesn't have the sense God gave her, not to go turning cartwheels in manure? But the Lord must truly protect the ignorant, because she came up with clean hands and shoes. A miracle, if I ever heard of one. Got herself a boyfriend out of it, too.*

Mom had been embarrassed then. She'd refused to go into the Pickford Farmers' Exchange for a whole year. She'd boycotted anything to do with Farm Bureau until she was out of high school.

"I think she was even kind of mad we insisted on inviting everyone on council to her wedding," Gram had chuckled.

Lori had always liked that story. She liked imagining Mom so much younger, turning cartwheels and falling in love. It made her seem more like Lori—not like someone who belonged in hotels and up at podiums.

It also made it seem like maybe someday Lori might be able to cartwheel into someone's heart and fall in love herself.

But Mom must not remember anything at all about turning those cartwheels and Pop embarrassing her. Because if she did, she wouldn't be going around the country telling everyone horrible stories about Lori.

Someone knocked on the door.

"Lori?" Mom called softly.

Even though the door was locked, Lori scrunched back against the tub.

"What?" she said.

"If it bothers you so much, I'll stop telling any stories about you," Mom said. "I'll cut you out of all of my speeches."

Lori wondered why she didn't feel the least bit triumphant. She felt almost rejected instead. Didn't Mom *want* to talk about Lori?

Lori reminded herself Mom was giving in; Lori had won. She stood up and opened the door a crack.

"Promise?" she asked.

Mom nodded. "I—I remember being fourteen," Mom said. "I remember how things can seem . . . out of proportion."

Oh, so Lori was wrong to be upset? So Lori was just silly and sensitive? The anger flared again.

"What about the other kids? Chuck and Mike and Joey and Emma?" Lori asked. "Will you stop talking about them, too?"

Mom winced. Lori could tell Mom hadn't thought of that.

"They haven't asked me to," Mom said stiffly.

"Mike and Joey and Emma haven't exactly had a chance, have they?" Lori asked. "They don't even know you're talking about them."

"They're young enough that I can still judge for them," Mom said.

Lori didn't know what made her push the issue. If

Mom had only said, *I know how you feel. I got mad when Pop spread stories about me, too. Let me tell you about some cartwheels. . . .* But Mom would never tell Lori the cartwheel story because it involved Daddy, and Mom didn't talk about Daddy.

"Chuck's here," Lori said. "He heard your speech. Hey, Chuck. What do you think?"

Chuck was sitting on the far bed now, watching TV. He pulled his attention away from a soap commercial.

"Huh?" he said.

"Isn't it unfair how Mom's been telling stories about us in all her speeches, and she's been doing it for years, and we didn't even know?" Lori fought to control her voice, but it was useless. She was crying again.

"Well, that was certainly an unbiased account of the situation," Mom said dryly. "Lori has asked me not to mention her in my speeches again, and we were wondering if you felt the same way."

Lori glared at Mom. How could she stay so calm? She sounded as formal as the queen of England, ordering tea.

She really must not care, Lori thought.

Chuck looked from Mom to Lori and back again. He squinted, looking as confused as if they'd both been speaking foreign languages. Lori had seen hogs make up their minds faster than Chuck did.

Finally he shrugged.

"I don't care," he said. "I, um, thought your speech was real good."

Then he looked back at the TV, as though it were dangerous to look at Mom or Lori for very long.

"Well," Mom said. "That's settled."

There was nothing left for Lori to do except stomp back into the bathroom and do her best to slam the door.

Chuck

The televised images danced in front of Chuck's eyes, but he wasn't seeing them.

Lori asked me for something, he thought again and again. *Lori hasn't asked me for anything in eight years.*

If only he were smarter, he could understand what was going on. Mom and Lori were mad at each other. He knew that. Lori didn't want Mom talking about her. He knew that, too, but didn't understand. Lori wanted Chuck to tell Mom not to talk about him, either.

Why? Why did Lori care?

What Chuck saw now, instead of the TV, was huge tangles. The whole conversation he'd just had was like Pop's piles of old baling twine, knotted and snarled and impossible to sort out. He could picture very clearly the twisted loops of twine lying on the barn floor.

He'd just stepped in one of those loops, and gotten caught.

Now Lori will never forgive me, he thought.

Lori

Lori couldn't believe that, after everything that had happened the night before, Mom still wanted to get up and take them sight-seeing the next morning.

"Come on, sleepyheads," she urged when the alarm went off at seven. "You don't want to miss anything, do you? We have to be back at the airport by three this afternoon—this may be your last chance to see Chicago for the rest of your life."

Lori wanted to say, *So what?* but she just groaned and rolled over.

When she did get up, she had that unsteady, fragile feeling she always had the morning after she'd cried herself to sleep. She didn't have to look in the mirror to know that her eyes were swollen and ugly, her entire face puffy from all those tears. Neither Mom nor Chuck seemed to notice. While Mom was in the shower, Lori got the ice bucket and sneaked down the hall to fill it. Then, back in the room, she wrapped several cubes in a wash-cloth and pressed it on her eyelids. That was the only method she'd ever found that worked.

Lori couldn't remember when she'd started crying herself to sleep back home. It wasn't really that often—maybe once every couple of months. Sometimes it was because of something specific that happened—John McArthur totally ignored her at a Junior Leadership meeting, or she got a B- on her English essay, or Courtney Snyder told Mickey James that Brandi Wyland had said that Lori was the biggest flirt in the freshman class and that everyone hated her for it. Sometimes there wasn't any reason at all—Lori just felt like crying. And so she did, sobbing silently in her bed for hours, until her eyes ached, and her head ached, and she miserably fell asleep. She wondered if other girls did this. Maybe it was connected to puberty. Lori had been the last one of her friends to get her period; maybe they had all been crying themselves to sleep once a month for years and they'd just never told her.

Lori didn't want to ask.

Regardless, she'd gotten very good at treating and camouflaging swollen eyelids. Ten minutes of the ice treatment, a little extra mascara—even if she didn't feel normal, she looked okay.

Half an hour later, the huge mirror in the elevator assured her that she'd erased all signs of crying; the long brass panel at the checkout desk reflected back a face devoid of emotion.

That was just the look Lori wanted.

"Yes, yes, we'll be back for our luggage this afternoon," Mom was assuring a man in an official-looking suit. She turned back to Lori and Chuck. "Let's have breakfast here at the hotel, all right?"

She led them through a maze of halls. Lori was sure they'd walked an entire city block before they even got to the door of the restaurant.

How could anyone keep a place like this straight in her head? Lori felt a pang of homesickness for small buildings, square street grids, restaurants surrounded by only parking lots.

Mom seemed entirely at home.

"We can go out to the science museum when it opens at nine thirty, and then come back downtown for lunch. If there's time, we can shop a little at Water Tower Place—it's this huge, ritzy mall with all these incredibly expensive stores. I can't promise that we could afford anything, but it's kind of fun to look," Mom said while they waited to be seated.

Lori wasn't interested in science, and Chuck had practically flunked general biology last year. Lori looked around the hotel restaurant, wondering whether she should tell Mom that. She knew Chuck wouldn't speak up. Surely he was as intimidated by all the shiny brass and fancy chandeliers as Lori was.

"Table for three?" asked the waiter or host or whatever he was called. He had an accent that made the words sound foreign, even though they weren't.

"Yes, please," Mom said crisply. She was used to talking to people like that, and Lori didn't even know what they were called.

The waiter guy pulled out Lori's chair for her and placed her napkin on her lap. Lori tried not to giggle. Then he handed her a menu. The cheapest breakfast, cold cereal, was $6.95.

"We could have gone to McDonald's," Lori said.

"I know," Mom said. "But I wanted to treat you. You can go to McDonald's anytime you want at home."

"Not really," Lori said. "Gram and Pop always say it costs too much."

Mom didn't say anything.

"Anyhow, it's not like Pickford County only has a McDonald's," Lori continued. "We have a Burger King there now, too. And a Bob Evans."

"I know," Mom said. "I live there, too, remember?"

"Oh, sorry," Lori said. "It's easy to forget when you're never around."

Lori couldn't believe she'd actually said that. Maybe she hadn't—maybe the words were just throbbing in her head so strongly that she only thought she'd spoken them out loud. For a second, no one reacted, and she silently hoped, *I didn't say it. I didn't say it. Nobody heard.* But then Chuck's eyes bugged out, and two spots of angry color appeared on Mom's cheeks.

"We'll pretend," Mom said quietly, "that you didn't say that. That we haven't had this conversation. We don't need a repeat of last night."

That made everything worse. You couldn't have your house burn down and blithely say, *We'll pretend that never happened*. You couldn't murder someone and say, *Let's pretend you're still alive*. You couldn't be furious enough to scream and cry and rage for hours and still smile sweetly and say, *Aren't we such a nice, happy family?*

But hadn't Lori been doing that for years?

She looked up and saw that the waiter guy was still there. He was focusing intently on pouring water for all of them, as if that required every ounce of his concentration. He'd heard everything. Lori felt her face go red; she'd thought she'd cried herself out the night before, but a fresh supply of tears threatened under her eyelids as she watched the guy walk away. He probably couldn't wait to tell the other servers, *You won't believe the horrible family I've got over there*. Lori had broken one of Gram and Pop's biggest rules: "Don't air your dirty laundry in public." It was closely related to the main question they asked anytime one of the kids even threatened to do anything wrong: "What will people think?"

Mom and Chuck were studying their menus now with every bit as much concentration as the waiter had used on the water.

"Are you feeling brave today, Chuck?" Mom asked with what had to be fake heartiness. "Want to try the salsa omelette?"

Chuck looked as startled as a bull hit with an electric prod.

"I—I thought I'd just have bacon and eggs," he said.

"Fine," Mom said. "Lori?"

"Cereal," Lori said.

"Are you sure?" Mom said. "We're going to be doing a lot of walking this morning. I don't want you getting too hungry—"

"Pop says a fool and his money are soon parted," Lori said self-righteously. She didn't know what had gotten into her; she hadn't meant to say that. She'd seen a movie once where a man was incapable of lying, and it got him into lots of trouble. She'd thought the movie was totally idiotic. But he'd been under a curse or something. What was Lori's excuse?

"Pop isn't—" Mom stopped. "Okay. Get whatever you want." Now her face was redder than Lori's. At least the waiter guy wasn't lingering over them anymore, listening intently while he pretended not to.

Another man came and took their orders. Mom asked for cereal, too. Lori wondered what *that* meant. She felt guilty and didn't know why.

Then the waiter went away, and the three of them were left alone with nothing to say. All of them kept taking sips of their water.

"Do you think the science museum is a good idea?" Mom finally asked. "I've been there a couple times, and it's really cool, but if there's something else you'd like better—I have the guidebook. . . ."

She was fumbling with her purse.

"Why don't we skip the museum and just go shopping?" Lori said.

"All right," Mom said evenly. "Is that okay with you, Chuck?"

Chuck nodded like one of those toy dogs with a spring for a neck.

"Fine," Mom said grimly. "I'm sure we'll have fun."

At least Mom can still lie, Lori thought.

Chuck

Chuck didn't get Lori.

Back home, she was Ms. Everything: honor roll student, high scorer on the freshman girls' basketball team, secretary of the church youth group, president of their 4-H club, even though that title usually went to a junior or senior. And most of all, she always seemed to know the right thing to say. Or, at least, the most popular thing to say.

Chuck knew how she and her friends talked, when it was just them and they didn't think anyone else was listening: "Did you see Suzanne's hair? I think she stuck her finger in an electric socket!" "Doesn't Brad Knisley stink?" "Can you believe it? They changed the seating assignments in algebra, and I'm stuck with dogbreath right behind me!"

But even then, Lori was usually the one saying,

"Stop! That's really nasty!" And in public—well, she might as well have a halo. Chuck remembered one time at school when he'd seen a girl crying at the back of the auditorium during an all-school assembly. He'd just stood there, wondering what to do. Did she need help? Or did she just want to be left alone? Chuck had decided to pretend not to see her, mainly because he didn't know what else to do. But five minutes later, he'd looked back, and there was Lori with her arm around the girl's shoulder, talking to her. The girl was nodding and even smiling a little through her tears.

Later, walking down the lane from where the school bus dropped them off, Chuck had gotten up the nerve to ask what the girl had been crying about. Lori had just given him a look.

"Chuck, that was Janice Seaver," Lori said.

The name didn't mean anything to Chuck.

"You know," Lori said impatiently. "It was her brother who was killed in that crash yesterday. The one we were having the assembly for."

"Oh," Chuck said, feeling dumb as dirt. "I didn't know."

And then Lori had run on ahead, because she had a lot of homework, and Chuck didn't have a chance to ask any of the other questions he wondered about: *What did you say to her? How did you know she wanted you to talk to her?* And most of all, *Would you cry if I was the dead one?*

Back home, the worst thing Lori ever did was ignore

Chuck. And nobody noticed that—or maybe nobody expected teenaged brothers and sisters to get along, anyway.

So everyone in Pickford County thought Lori was the greatest. The old ladies at church always nodded approvingly while they watched Lori scrub down tables at the annual ice-cream social. "What a good kid," they murmured. "What a hard worker."

And the parents who dropped her off from baby-sitting always came in and told Gram and Pop, "She is such a nice girl."

So why was she being so mean to Mom?

It had started last night, after Mom's speech. Or during it. It was really rude of Lori to get up and leave right in the middle.

Then she and Mom had that fight afterward. . . .

Chuck didn't want to think about his part in it.

Breakfast was hard, because there was still that strange tension in the air. Lori would say something, or Mom would say something, and they'd just smirk at each other.

It was like watching a war.

Chuck watched the chandeliers instead. The millions of tiny prisms were so graceful, dangling from the lights like glass waterfalls. He wondered about the people who got to make things like that—surely there were people involved? Surely something that beautiful wasn't stamped out by some assembly-line machine, the same way as tractor parts or silo frames?

A crazy idea sprouted in Chuck's head, but he stomped it down, squashed it dead. He was fat, stupid Chuck Lawson. People like him weren't entitled to dreams.

Now they were at Water Tower Place, Chuck trailing along behind Mom and Lori as they moved from store to store. Chuck studied the pattern in the tiles on the floor, paying only enough attention to Mom and Lori to make sure he didn't lose them.

They were still fighting.

"Well, why do you have to talk like that during your speeches?" Lori said on the threshold of Marshall Field's. "'Now, listen up, all you honey chiles, and ah'm a'gonna tell you a ni-ice story,'" she mocked in a southern accent as thick as oil.

"I *don't* talk like that," Mom snapped.

"Maybe not quite that bad," Lori conceded. "But you get this accent when you're making speeches, like you're some hick from the sticks. It sounds bad."

Mom didn't answer. They walked into the juniors' department.

"What do you think of that dress?" Mom said. "If you found something you really liked, we could get your prom dress for next year."

"Mom, sophomores don't go to the prom," Lori said. She looked at Chuck, like she expected him to back her up.

Chuck probably wouldn't ever go to prom.

"I know," Mom said, fingering another dress. "I just thought, if an older boy asked you . . ."

"You trying to marry me off young or something?" Lori asked. "Get rid of me?"

Her tone was joking, but the edge was still there. Her voice made Chuck think of sheep being sheared: a sharp razor hidden in soft wool.

"No, I don't want you to marry young," Mom said steadily. "I don't think marrying young is a good idea at all." She wasn't looking at dresses anymore but straight at Lori, with a very serious expression on her face.

"You were only eighteen when you and Dad got married," Lori said, sneering. "So you regret marrying him?"

Chuck froze, and even Lori had the grace to look ashamed. Her look of scorn slid into one of uncertainty, like she hadn't known what she was going to say and was stunned herself that she'd said it.

Chuck sneaked a look at Mom, and her expression was frozen, too. It was like the pictures in Chuck's world history book of the people caught by the lava, centuries ago. Stuck for all time.

Then, "No, of course I don't regret marrying your father," Mom said in a careful tone. "But sometimes I wish . . ." Her voice trailed off. She was staring past the mannequins. Then she looked back at Lori. "Well, you can always wish lots of things, can't you? It's like Pop says, 'If wishes were horses, then beggars could ride.'"

Chuck never had understood that saying.

They left Marshall Field's without buying any dresses.

They went to another store.

Chuck liked the open middle section of the mall, but being in the stores themselves made him feel strange, like he wasn't getting enough air to breathe. Didn't these people ever long to see even a blade of grass? Something real?

Lori and Mom were fighting about something else now.

"I just want to know, why'd you have to go and name me Lori?" Lori asked. "It sounds like somebody's mother. Why not Courtney or Brittany or Brandi? Something like the other kids?"

"Your father liked the name Lori," Mom said softly, and that shut Lori up.

"Why did you name me Chuck?" Chuck said, before he could stop himself.

Mom and Lori both turned to look at him, like they'd forgotten he was along.

"You were named for Pop," Mom said. "Charles Frederick."

"Oh," Chuck said, retreating. He *knew* he was named for Pop. Didn't Pop remind him of that all the time? "Don't know how someone named for me could forget to grind feed. . . . Don't know how my own namesake could forget to do night work." What Chuck had really meant to say was, *Why Chuck? Why not Charles or Charlie or even—* Chuck had heard this nickname once on TV—*Chas?* Chuck imagined he would somehow have been a different person, if only he'd gotten a different name. As a name, Chuck was pale and pasty and flabby—a fat boy without a spine. Buckteeth and a burr haircut. Chuck. A Chas or a Charlie would be popular, everybody's pal. A Charles would be dignified somehow. A true Charles would be somebody.

Chuck couldn't possibly be a Charles.

But then, neither could Pop. He'd gone by his middle name since he was born.

"Do you mind all this shopping, Chuck?" Mom asked. "You've got to be bored silly. Are there any stores you want to look at? Any clothes you need?"

"No," Chuck said, looking at the floor. "But would you mind if—?" The racks of clothing pressed in around him. Was Mom offering him a chance to escape? "Would it be okay if I went off by myself for a little bit? I could meet you wherever you want me to be by lunchtime."

"Well . . ." Mom hesitated. Chuck could tell she was thinking about Lori disappearing the night before. He hoped she was thinking, *But that was Lori, and this is Chuck. And Chuck's a boy. It's not so dangerous for him.*

It was strange for Chuck to even hope that people would see him as more responsible than Lori.

"Okay," Mom decided. "Meet us, um, back at this fountain at twelve thirty."

Lori gave Chuck a look like she wished she were the one splitting off. Chuck felt triumphant. *I got something and Lori didn't!* Now, that was a first.

He walked out of the mall into the fresh air. Actually, the air wasn't all that fresh, and there still wasn't a blade of grass in sight. But Chuck could see the sky now.

The sidewalk was crowded, but nobody paid the slightest bit of attention to Chuck. Chuck liked that. Everyone ignored him at school, too, but that was a different kind of ignoring—it was like they were all just pretending to ignore him, so they could jump all over him and make fun of him as soon as he did something dumb.

Chuck decided he didn't want to think about school right now.

He watched the faces of the people coming toward him. Nobody smiled and said, *Hi,* like they always did in town back home, but most people looked pleasant enough. Gram had warned him about big cities: "Your mom doesn't think a thing about it, but they've got muggers who will rob you blind, right in broad daylight, and no one will even stop to call the police." Chuck patted his front pocket, where he'd tucked a twenty-dollar bill. But his jeans were so tight, it would take some real doing to get that money away from him. He wasn't going to worry.

Chuck wandered carelessly for a while, crossing the street when he had the light, turning the corner when he didn't. He didn't have a destination in mind. He was just glad to be away from home, away from Mom and Lori's strange fight. He didn't dare hope for anything else.

But then he walked under an elevated train track, and a building appeared in front of him. It was like a miracle or a mirage or magic. He read the words carved in stone three times, because he couldn't quite believe his eyes.

He had walked right up to the Art Institute of Chicago. An art museum.

If anyone had asked him if he'd wanted to go there, he would have said no. If he'd even known it existed, he would have veered in the other direction. But being there was enough of an invitation.

Breathing fast, Chuck began climbing the stone steps.

Lori

Another airplane.

Lori marveled at how familiar everything seemed: the pull-down table, the tiny window with its miniature shade, the button that lowered the seat back, the flight attendant demonstrating how to use the oxygen mask. This was only her second flight, but already she felt like an old pro at flying.

She was seated on the aisle this time. She looked up and down the other rows, and everyone else seemed comfortable with flying, too. It was weird to think that all Lori's life, when she'd been going about her usual routine—doing algebra homework, watering the 4-H hogs, washing the dishes for Gram—there had been all these people in the air above her. It was another world.

Mom's world.

Lori never really thought much about where Mom was

when she away—she was either home or she wasn't. And when she wasn't home, she didn't exist.

But that wasn't how Lori had always thought of things. She could remember years and years and years ago, the first few trips Mom took. Then, Lori had asked Gram every five minutes, "Where's Mommy now? What's Mommy doing now?" She could almost see herself, maybe seven years old, sitting on the kitchen floor playing with her Barbies while Gram pulled loaves of bread out of the oven. Her hair stuck out in two ponytails on either side of her head, and she was asking Gram, "Is Mom cooking supper right now, too? What's she going to have for supper?"

And every night after Gram tucked her into bed, she'd lay in the dark, vowing, "I'm not going to sleep until Mommy comes home. If I stay awake, she'll come home now." When Mom was away, it was like there was always some part of Lori tensed and waiting, even when she was at school, when she wouldn't have seen Mom anyway.

She'd been at school when Daddy died.

But Gram promised that Mom was coming home. Gram said Mommy was just taking a short trip, and then she'd be back, and she'd probably never go away again.

Only, Mom kept going away. Her one night a month turned into a couple days every other week. And that turned into a week away for every week at home. Now it seemed weird when Mom was home for a whole week at a time.

Not that Lori really paid attention.

Lori remembered the exact moment she'd stopped

caring. It was a night years and years ago, when Mom got home late, after bedtime. Lori was still awake, and Mom came in to give her a good-night kiss. Lori should have thrown her arms around Mom's neck and whispered, *I missed you. I love you. I'm so glad you're home.* But Lori squeezed her eyes shut and pretended to be asleep.

She'd already gotten a good-night kiss from Gram. She didn't need another one.

Now Lori sneaked a glance over at Mom, in the middle seat. Mom had her head back and her eyes closed, and Lori wondered if she might have even fallen asleep. Every few seconds she winced, as if she had a headache or bad dreams.

Lori figured she was responsible for any headache Mom had. And probably the bad dreams, too.

You ought to be ashamed of yourself, Lori thought to herself, but it was Gram's voice she heard in her head: *I didn't raise you to be rude.* If it really had been Gram talking, she would have thrown in a Bible verse, too— about disobedient children getting what they deserve.

I wasn't disobedient, Lori thought. *I was just . . . curious. I was just asking questions.*

But she knew how she'd sounded, all day long. Even Chuck had been giving her strange looks. Lori went to school with some kids who believed in demon possession—*really* believed in it, brought it up every time there was any in-class discussion—and Lori briefly wondered if she could blame that. She thought about touching Mom on the arm and apologizing: *I don't know why I was such a brat today. I'm sorry. Maybe I was possessed by demons.*

Maybe she would have apologized—not with the excuse, just flat out—if Mom had really answered any of her questions. But she hadn't. She'd changed the subject, she'd evaded, she'd given those one-sentence half replies: "No, I don't want you to marry young." "No, I don't regret marrying your dad." "Your father liked the name Lori." They were answers that pushed Lori away. They built walls, not windows.

They made Lori angrier than ever.

The plane was taking off now. Mom opened her eyes and leaned away from Lori, pointing out sights on the ground to Chuck. Their heads totally blocked the view for Lori, but she didn't care. She hated Chicago. She'd been terrible there. Her face burned just thinking about it.

She thought about what her friends would ask her when she got home: *Was the shopping great? Were the guys cute? Did you have fun?* And she'd give the same kind of nonanswers Mom had given her.

Suddenly Lori wished fervently that she was back home with her friends, right now. She could be on the phone gossiping about Jackie Stires's pool party, figuring out whose parents could drive them to the movies on Saturday night. Everything at home seemed so simple suddenly. There were rules there. You cleaned up after yourself. You didn't flirt with other girls' boyfriends. You ignored Mike and Joey's roughhousing unless it looked like they were going to break something. You kept your eyes on your own paper when you were taking tests at school. You said, "Please" and "Thank you," and you didn't tell anyone what you were really thinking.

Why had Lori suddenly felt there were no rules in Chicago?

She winced as the plane turned sharply, knocking her against the arm of her seat. Then the plane leveled off, following a straight path.

They were on their way to Atlanta now. Maybe Atlanta would be better.

Chuck

Mom had gotten Chuck those airsickness bracelets, and he had them on, but it didn't matter: there was no way he could be sick now. He wasn't even scared, and here he was, staring straight down at the ground, thousands of feet below him.

If I die now, I wouldn't care. I would die happy, he thought. But he would care. There was a whole world he'd discovered today, and he intended to see more of it.

Come on, plane, don't go down, he thought, as if he could help the pilots. But the plane was in no danger of going down. It climbed up and up and up, until all he could see was clouds.

"Pretty cool, huh?" Mom said beside him.

Chuck nodded. Suddenly he wanted to tell Mom where he'd gone today. But he couldn't. When she'd asked, when they met back at the water fountain in the mall, he'd just said, "Oh, I just wandered around. Saw the city." And then Lori had said something nasty, and Mom got distracted, so he didn't say anything else. Which was fine. He didn't want anyone ruining the day for him. He could just hear Lori: *You went to the art museum? Why?*

Never in a million years could he have explained to Lori what it had been like to stand in front of those paintings and *feel* what the artist had been trying to show him. He'd seen paintings before, of course—copies of them, anyway. One of the kids in their 4-H club had that lady with the strange smile—Mona something . . . Mona Lisa?—hanging up in their bathroom. In their bathroom! But that whole family was kind of weird. The dad was a professor at some college an hour away. Everybody knew professors and people who commuted that far weren't normal.

What Chuck had seen in the art museum was different from looking at some lady's picture hanging over a toilet. At the art museum, the paintings were treated reverently—framed just so, hung just so, lighted just so. And people practically tiptoed around.

At first, Chuck had been afraid that someone would tell him he didn't belong, maybe even kick him out. He'd practically trembled when he paid his money at the front desk. He waited for the thin, dry-looking man to push his sweaty twenty-dollar bill back and sniff, *No hicks allowed.* But the man only made change and handed him a brochure, and Chuck was free to look at whatever he wanted.

He didn't see any other farm boys in jeans and John Deere T-shirts walking around, but nobody seemed to care. One of the security guards even gave him an encouraging nod as he walked from room to room.

Chuck had stood in front of a big red painting for a long time. It was the kind of thing that Gram and Pop would have mocked as "modern art." They'd seen something like it on TV once, and Pop had scoffed, "Did some kindergartener make that?" But Chuck felt like he was falling into the color, it was so intense. And he, Chuck Lawson, who never understood anything at school, understood that painting.

"Like it?" a voice said.

For the first time, Chuck noticed a man standing beside him. He had a goatee and a ponytail. Pop would have scoffed at him, too. Chuck was afraid the man was making fun of him—as if someone with a ponytail could never see someone like Chuck liking a painting like that. But the man looked serious.

"Yes," Chuck said simply.

"Good," the man said.

And that was all, but it was the best conversation Chuck had had in years.

Lori

Mom had more to do in Atlanta than she had in Chicago.

"I'm busy until four o'clock today, and then there's the banquet this evening," she said over breakfast. (They were eating at McDonald's. Did that mean something?) "Will you two be okay on your own?"

"Sure," Lori said.

"Oh, yeah," Chuck said.

Was it just Lori's imagination, or did he sound enthusiastic? Chuck never sounded enthusiastic about anything.

"Well, try to stick together," Mom said, almost nervously, wiping the remains of an Egg McMuffin from her lips with a napkin. "This is a big city, you know."

"We *know*," Lori said, too sharply. Mom gave her a look but didn't say anything. Lori instantly wanted to apologize. That was silly, though—why should she apologize for saying, "We know"?

Lori wondered if Mom didn't really have that much more to do in Atlanta. Maybe she was just tired of hanging out with Lori and Chuck.

Lori wouldn't blame her.

But Mom had explained that this was a convention of people who gave speeches; Mom was here to talk about how to speak in public. Lori had seen the brochure herself—Mom was leading seminars called "Why Should Anyone Listen to *Me*? Figuring Out Your Message" and "It's Mine, All Mine: Capturing an Audience's Attention." And she was giving the keynote address at the banquet that night. So Mom wasn't lying when she said she'd be busy.

Lori should probably be impressed that all these people who gave speeches would want to listen to Mom. But she couldn't help wondering, *Why did Mom bring us along if she's just going to work?*

They went back to the hotel room and Mom left for the conference. Lori brushed her teeth. The whole day stretched ahead of her like an empty calendar page.

"Want to go to the Coke museum with me?" she asked Chuck through a mouthful of bubbles. She spit in the sink. "The hotel guidebook says Coke was invented here, and they have a museum showing the entire history. At the end, they let you drink all the Coke you want."

She felt so virtuous asking Chuck to go somewhere with her. Maybe that was how she could make up for being so nasty to Mom. She'd be nice to Chuck all day long—no matter how hard that was. She wouldn't even think about the possibility that someone might mistake them for girlfriend and boyfriend. (Okay, she'd already thought of it. But she wouldn't think about it again.) It'd be like . . . paying back God. By the end of the day, her conscience would feel as clean as her teeth.

But, "No," Chuck said slowly. "I've got other plans."

Plans? Chuck had plans? In a city he'd never stepped foot in before in his entire life?

"Oh," Lori said. "Um. Okay." She hesitated. Her conscience was at stake here, after all. "But didn't Mom want us to stay together? Can I—?" She was out on a limb now. But she kept going. "Can I go with you?"

She was almost pleading. Chuck looked panicked.

"No, no. You'd be bored. Or something." He gulped. "And Mom didn't say we *had* to stay together."

Lori's pride prevented her from truly begging. She was practically speechless, anyway. What could Chuck be up to?

"Well," Chuck said. "Guess I'll be going. See you later."

"Yeah," Lori said.

He tucked his plastic credit card-like hotel key in his pocket and went out the door. Lori stared after him. The door shut in her face.

"Okay. Fine," Lori said.

She grabbed her own key and went out the door behind him.

She didn't really intend to follow him, but when her elevator arrived in the lobby, she saw him just going out the front door. She ducked behind a flower arrangement bigger than the outhouse Pop still kept out by the barn. And then, when she felt sure Chuck hadn't seen her, she inched across the gleaming marble floor and went through the revolving door herself.

Chuck was tall as well as big—at fifteen, he'd already topped six feet—so it was easy keeping his dark head in sight. She bumped into people once or twice and almost stepped out into traffic at a busy intersection when Chuck crossed on a yellow light. But he never looked back, so she stopped worrying about being spotted.

All the way, she kept playing guessing games with herself about where he was actually going. The Olympic Park? One of the sports stadiums? Chuck had never cared about sports. He wouldn't even play in the softball games they always had before 4-H meetings in the summer.

But maybe that was just because the other kids laughed at him running the bases. Mike and Joey imitated him: "Look at me! I'm the Michelin tire man!" "Oh no, I'm shaking the ground!"

Lori thought back—what about when Chuck was younger? When he wasn't fat? For a second, she caught a fleeting memory of her and Chuck and their dad playing catch in the backyard of their old house. Hadn't Chuck been whining, "I don't want it to hit me! It'll hurt!"? And their dad had insisted, "Look, it's a *soft*ball. You won't get hurt. Just catch it."

She wasn't sure if that was something she truly remembered or something she'd dreamed. Or just plain made up.

Regardless, Chuck didn't like sports now.

The zoo? Chuck didn't like animals. Pop had to remind him a million times a day to feed the hogs.

The CNN tour? Chuck hated watching the news.

Really, Lori couldn't think of anything Chuck liked.

He turned a corner and went into a glitzy, glass building. The sign said, HIGH MUSEUM OF ART.

Art? *Art?*

Lori looked again, almost certain she'd misread the sign. But, no. That's what it said. Maybe the sign went with a different building. She actually went over and peered in a window. A sculpture of a little boy looked back at her, and a painting hung over his head.

Chuck had gone into an art museum.

He didn't come back out, so Lori knew it wasn't a matter of just using the bathroom.

Was it possible that Chuck *liked* art?

Lori didn't know anybody who liked art. Plenty of her friends' mothers did crafts—decoupaging picnic baskets, stenciling Christmas cards, needlepointing little signs with sayings like "A moment on the lips, an eternity on the hips." But crafts weren't art.

Back when they were in elementary school, they'd had an art teacher come in once a week. She was old and smelled bad, and she'd yelled at Lori once for taking two sheets of green construction paper instead of one. (Lori hadn't even known she'd taken two—they stuck together.) She mostly had them cut out things—

construction-paper leaves in the fall, construction-paper wreaths at Christmas, construction-paper flowers for Mother's Day. (Lori gave hers to Gram, because what was Mom going to do with them?) But there wasn't even an art teacher in high school, not since the last school levy failed.

So if Chuck had liked art all along, there was no way anyone would have known.

Lori started laughing. *Chuck likes art! Chuck likes* art*!*

Other people on the sidewalk were giving her strange looks and dodging around her. She sat down on a concrete ledge and kept laughing. Chuck liked art! She didn't usually make fun of Chuck back home, preferring the "Ignore him and maybe he'll go away" approach. But this was too funny not to share. She got up and went into the art museum; as she suspected, she could get to the museum gift shop without paying the admission fee. She bought a postcard with some armless sculpture on the front and wrote on it before she even left the shop:

Dear Angie,
    Guess what? My big brother (and I do mean big) has a secret obsession. He's been sneaking out to visit . . . art museums. Weird, huh?
    I'm fine. Miss you. Can't wait to catch up on all the gossip when I get home.
    Love,
    Lori

Lori didn't have a stamp, so she tucked the postcard in her purse to mail later. She started walking out of the museum, but she looked back at the last minute, suddenly curious about what Chuck might possibly see in an art museum, anyway. Through the entryway to the main part of the museum, she could see half of a strange painting of someone with three eyes and two noses and a bluish face. It didn't even look as good as the amateur paintings at the fine arts exhibit at the county fair.

But Chuck was standing in front of it. His back was to Lori, so she watched him watching the picture. He was absolutely still; he didn't so much as scratch his nose. He had the same posture the minister had before the altar at church, breaking Communion bread: straight, erect, reverent. And Chuck *never* stood up straight. He always slumped, his shoulders hunched over as if that would pull his T-shirt forward to hide his fat belly.

Lori started giggling again, so she rushed out the museum door. But, out on the sidewalk again, she stopped laughing. This was weird. Maybe she didn't want to send the postcard to Angie after all. Having Chuck be that weird might make Lori seem weird, too.

Lori started walking down the street, suddenly wanting to get away from the art museum. But she didn't know where else to go. The thought of going to the Coke museum all by herself wasn't appealing at all. She knew how it would be: all these other families and clusters of friends and then Lori, by herself, with no one to mutter back and forth with: *They make how much Coke a day? Did you ever think it looked like that being mixed up?*

Lori wandered down another street, aimlessly, hoping she'd see something else to catch her interest. She had money for shopping, after all; she had the whole day to do with as she wished. Lori tried to convince herself that that was a luxury, but she just felt forlorn. She had nothing to do and nobody to do it with.

Lori wasn't used to being alone. At home, she complained about it: "Why do I have to share my room with Emma?" "Why can't Joey leave me alone while I'm doing homework?" "Gram, can't you just stop chattering about your tomato preserves for five seconds?" (She'd never actually asked the last question—just thought it.) And at school, more happily, she always traveled in a crowd of friends. She could always count on having Angie or Breanna walking beside her, or Dana or Chelsea sitting behind her in class, passing notes when the teacher wasn't looking. It would be horrible to be alone at school.

It was worse in a strange city. Lori felt totally invisible, unnoticed. Nobody knew who she was. She didn't matter to anyone here.

But that's what Mom was all the time—alone in a strange city. What kind of a life was that?

For a minute, Lori was afraid that she'd asked the question out loud, because a black woman looked at her, then quickly looked away, just like Mom had looked at homeless people in Chicago. But Lori wasn't that out of it—she would know if she'd moved her lips, and she hadn't. She looked around.

She was the only white person in sight.

Something like panic started to rise up out of her gut, and she forced it down.

So you're the only white person. So what? It was getting close to lunchtime; the street was crowded. It was just a coincidence that this street was crowded with all black people. Except for Lori.

Maybe I'm in danger. No—I shouldn't think that. That's racist. Lori felt like she was in danger, anyway. Her heart pounded, and she could feel the adrenaline flooding her system. She wanted to run, but she was still calm enough not to want to look silly.

You're not in any danger. Calm down. But she didn't know that for sure. She wasn't used to big cities. For all she knew, she'd wandered into some notorious housing project, and there was going to be a shoot-out between rival gangs any minute.

There are nice stores all around you. These people are well dressed. Better dressed than Lori, actually. There were more Tommy Hilfiger and Nike logos than Lori had ever seen outside of a store before. Lori was staring so hard that she caught the eye of a teenaged girl walking past; the girl gave her a half smile and walked on.

Would she have smiled if I was about to be killed? Or assaulted? Abducted? Raped?

Lori started walking faster. In the next block, she saw a white man in a business suit. He didn't even look her way. And then in the next block, there were as many white people as black. Lori wasn't in any danger. She never had been.

She sank weakly onto a concrete bench, her heart still thumping unnaturally. Her new shirt was drenched with sweat. What was wrong with her? The worst thing anybody had done to her was smile.

But I was different. I was surrounded by people who weren't like me.

For no reason at all, Lori suddenly remembered something that had happened only the week before at a Junior Leadership meeting. Everyone was clowning around afterward, throwing water balloons and laughing about it. Lori was thrilled because Roger Stanton had aimed one right at her—did that maybe mean he liked her? It was a great game.

Then one of the water balloons hit Chuck.

Everyone got quiet. Chuck wasn't even out in the playing area. He was sitting alone on the ground by a fence, waiting for Gram to come and pick them up. Whoever hit him had to have been trying.

"Sorry," Mitch Turland said. "I'm real sorry."

Another water balloon slapped the ground by Chuck's feet and burst. Water splashed up in his face. Now he was soaked.

"Oops," Sam Shettles said. "Me, too."

Lori willed Chuck to laugh the whole thing off. *Grab a water balloon yourself and start throwing. Make a big joke of it,* she thought.

But Chuck didn't move. Another balloon zipped toward him, this one exploding against the fence rail right over his head. Chuck's face turned red under the dripping water.

No, no, Lori thought. *Whatever you do, don't cry.*

Gram had shown up in the pickup truck before anything else could happen. She'd made both of the kids get in the back because they were wet. Lori had sat there, the wind whipping hair into her face, the fireflies starting to rise over the cornfields on either side of the road. And she was just furious with Chuck.

"Don't you know how to play along?" she yelled at him.

He didn't answer.

And Lori couldn't understand him at all.

But now—Lori remembered her panic, just a few moments ago, at being different. Had the Junior Leadership meeting felt that way to Chuck? Was that how he felt all the time, in all those places Lori felt accepted and admired—all the places she belonged?

Slowly, Lori reached into her purse and pulled out the postcard she'd intended to send to Angie. She ripped it in half, then ripped it again. And again. She kept going until it was shredded, like confetti.

Chuck

Chuck forgot to eat lunch.

He would have forgotten about meeting Mom at four, too, except that at three forty-five polite chimes echoed through the art museum and a classy-sounding voice announced, "We regret to inform the patrons of the High Museum of Art that we will be closing early today, due to our air-conditioning problems."

Chuck hadn't even noticed that they were having air-conditioning problems.

But the announcement forced him to look at his watch, then he took off running. Fifteen minutes. Could he get back to the hotel in fifteen minutes?

He got turned around leaving the art museum and went the wrong way for three blocks. Fortunately, the round top of the hotel stuck up high above the buildings around it, so he navigated his way back looking up the whole time.

His watch said 3:57 when he stepped onto the elevator. He was going to make it!

Of course, Lori would probably tattle on him, anyway, for not staying with her. He gulped. He never got in trouble with Mom. But the art museum had been worth it. He closed his eyes briefly, and visions swam before his eyes—colors and strokes, portraits that revealed more than photographs, landscapes that made him long to travel everywhere.

The elevator dinged on his floor and he hurried to the room. The door was just swinging shut.

Mom was already back.

He rushed in behind her, wondering how he could explain. How he could counter whatever Lori had already told Mom.

Mom had her back to Chuck.

"Where's your brother?" she was asking. "Don't tell me you two got separated. I thought I very specifically said—"

Lori looked past Mom to Chuck.

"Couldn't you find the ice machine?" she said. "It's right down the hall."

"Um—um—," Chuck sputtered.

"Oh, you forgot the ice bucket. Stupid!" Lori's voice was teasing. But she flashed a defiant look at Mom.

Chuck tried to figure out what was going on. Wasn't Lori going to tell on him?

Mom turned and looked back apologetically at Chuck.

"I'm sorry," she said. "I was jumping to conclusions. I

never said you had to tie your wrists together just to go get ice."

She slid out of her high-heeled shoes and collapsed onto the nearest bed.

"I am all talked out," she moaned. "How was your day? What did you two do?"

"Just looked around some," Lori said. "Saw the city."

Chuck squinted at Lori in confusion. She was covering for him. Why? She flashed him a look that very clearly said, *Keep your mouth shut.* Mom didn't even notice because her eyes were closed.

"Hmm," Mom said. "Where did you eat lunch?"

"Wendy's," Lori said smoothly.

Chuck had never known Lori was such a good liar. Maybe she wasn't lying. Maybe she really had eaten at Wendy's. Only, she was making Mom think Chuck had been there with her.

His stomach growled.

"After lunch, it was so hot, we just came back here and swam in the pool," Lori said.

Lori looked him straight in the eye, daring him to contradict her.

She knew.

WHAT JOAN LAWSON WANTED TO SAY
DURING HER SPEECH IN ATLANTA:

I don't feel like talking about time and the importance of living each day to its fullest. I want to talk about my kids.

Something has happened. Something has changed.

Chuck is still off in his own little world, but he sits there smiling when he thinks no one is watching him.

Chuck—smiling?

Why?

And Lori—well, I won't tell you how Lori behaved in Chicago. I'm ashamed. And I'm ashamed of myself for not telling her so.

But here . . . in Atlanta . . . Okay, she's still not really talking to me. But she and Chuck have something going on. They had a good day together. They're actually speaking to each other.

Maybe I was mistaken about the purpose of this trip. Maybe I expected too much, thinking I could mend my relationship with them. Maybe the best I can hope for from this trip is that Lori and Chuck can be friends with each other again. Like they used to be.

What does my broken heart matter, if theirs are whole?

I can remember them at three and four: overall straps sliding off their shoulders, bare feet covered in mud, sticks clutched in their hands like fishing rods. Lori, who always spoke for both of them, would announce, "Me and Chuck are catching supper."

It didn't matter where they were—haymow, hog barn, tractor seat, cow pasture—Lori and Chuck were there together. Back then, I don't think one of them would take a breath without telling the other one first.

When did that change? With school? No—I can remember them waiting for the school bus together, hand in hand. It was after that.

I think I know when they stopped being friends. I just don't know why.

It was the funeral.

If you saw what I see in my mind, you'd cry. A little boy and a little girl standing beside their father's freshly dug grave. The coffin has been lowered in, the minister has said his last "Amen." Everyone's leaving. The widow, her stomach huge with her fifth child, is trying to tell the children it's time to go.

"Come on, Chuck. Come on, Lori," she says, trying to

keep the tears out of her voice. "We need to go pick up Joey and Mikey at Aunt Louise's house."

"No," the little girl says.

The girl's grandparents talk to her. Aunts and uncles plead with her. Even the funeral director bends down on his knee in the mud and assures her that it's okay to leave her father's body right there in the ground, alone.

"The part of him that matters is in heaven now," the funeral director says. "He's happy now."

"I'm staying here with Daddy," the girl says.

The minister comes back and tries to talk kindergarten theology, but his pleas are useless, too. The mother knows what has to be done. But, newly widowed and vastly pregnant, she doesn't have it in her to drag a six-year-old kicking and screaming from her father's grave.

We used Chuck instead.

You should have seen him then. It's hard to remember now, but he was scrawny beyond words. Small for his age. Heartbreakingly thin. We coached him like a little windup doll, and he went over to stand by Lori.

"Daddy wants you to go home," he said. "Come on."

That thin, reedy, little-boy voice. So brave. A person could cry for days, just remembering that voice.

Lori sneaked her hand into Chuck's. He bent his head toward her ear and they whispered, back and forth. And then, slowly, they began walking away from the grave.

If I live to be one hundred, I'll see them like that forever. Hand in hand. Lori was wearing her leftover Easter *dress. Pink. Her hair was in ringlets with a big white bow. Chuck had his hair slicked back; he had blue suspenders holding up his checked pants.*

Those were not funeral clothes. They don't make funeral clothes for six- and seven-year-olds.

After a few minutes, Lori broke away from Chuck. She ran ahead and beat everyone else back to the car.

That's the last time I remember seeing them hand in hand or whispering or acting like they cared about each other at all.

Of course, they're teenagers now. Teenaged siblings don't hold hands.

Still.

Don't you wonder what they said?

I can't ask, of course. It's better for them if they don't remember.

WHAT JOAN LAWSON ACTUALLY SAID
DURING HER SPEECH IN ATLANTA:

Every speech has to come to an end.

I'm sure you've all heard speeches that *felt* interminable—I sincerely hope that this hasn't been one of them. [Big grin. Pause for laughter from the audience.] But in life, as in speeches, you don't want to be worrying about what you've left unsaid. When you reach that twenty-ninth minute of your half-hour speech, that's not the time to start thinking, *Oh no! I forgot to tell you . . .* We have only so much time in front of the microphone, just as we have only so much time on this earth. When the time comes for you to walk away from the great podium of life, do it with your head held high, your shoulders back, and the words of your best speech still ringing in everyone's ears.

Chicago. Atlanta. Philadelphia. Phoenix.

Lori felt numb.

I am not getting to know American cities, she thought. *I'm learning hotels. Restaurants. Airports.*

She was becoming an expert at using hotel blow-dryers. She could decipher airline departure/arrival charts without even trying. She was actually getting sick of eating burgers and fries. But she already had trouble remembering which city had had that great zoo Mom wanted them to see, which city had had the Coke museum Lori missed.

So what? Lori thought. *I didn't want to be here—any of the "here"s—anyway.*

At least she hadn't blown up at Mom again. Sometimes when Mom was talking to her, Lori could feel the muscles twitching in her face, as if her mouth had a mind of its own and was going to yell at Mom for her.

When that happened, Lori clenched her teeth, pressed her lips together, held everything in.

Sometimes Lori thought Mom was avoiding them; several times, even when she didn't have a speech to give, she'd sent Chuck and Lori out on their own: "I'm a little tired. Why don't you two go see Independence Hall and the Liberty Bell by yourselves?"

And then Chuck would scurry off to some art museum. And Lori would be alone.

She could have tattled. Whenever Mom was out of the room, it was always on the tip of Lori's tongue to taunt Chuck: *I know your secret.*

Back home, she wouldn't have thought it was worth her time to tease him. But traveling, all her reasons reversed. She was very careful around Chuck now, as if he were the one who knew a secret about her. Or as if he were stronger or smarter or better looking or more popular or more—*something*—than her.

The farther she got from Pickford County, the more she wondered, strangely, if somehow he was.

He had his art museums. What did she have?

Back home, she knew, there were people who were jealous of her. When the principal announced over the loudspeaker that she was a nominee for the Homecoming Court, the girl sitting behind Lori in English class had let out a deep sigh. She'd patted Lori's back and gushed, "You're a celebrity."

And after that, even after somebody else was voted

freshman attendant, the girl always looked at Lori admiringly. Lori couldn't pass her in the hall without feeling the girl's eyes on her back, all the way down the hall.

Lori just wished there were boys who looked at her like that.

In 4-H, she'd been selected as a camp counselor, even though most of the other counselors were juniors and seniors.

"We went by maturity, not chronological age," one of the members of the selection committee had confided to Gram in the hall, afterward. "You should be so proud of your granddaughter!"

Even in their own home, Lori always had Emma trailing after her, trying to do everything the same way as her. When Lori swept her hair up into a ponytail, so did Emma. When Lori sat at the kitchen table doing homework, Emma pulled out her second grade work sheets and traced her answers again and again, for as long as it took for Lori to finish.

Sometimes Lori missed Emma more than she'd have ever thought possible.

She missed everyone and everything about Pickford County that whispered to her a thousand times a day, *You're really something. You're something special.*

But special in Pickford County was nothing in the outside world.

She could walk down a single concourse in the Philadelphia airport and see a dozen girls prettier than her. Sitting on the airplane from Philadelphia to Phoenix, she heard a girl about her age switch from Spanish to English to a language Lori couldn't even identify, all in the space of three minutes.

Lori had aced Spanish I, but that just meant that she could say *"Yo hablo espanol"* with a straight face.

Lying in bed in one strange hotel after another, Lori found herself writing mental letters home that were entirely different from the "Having a great time!" post-cards she actually sent. *The world's a pretty big place, you know? . . . We flew over the Grand Canyon, and it's the biggest hole you could imagine. . . . The desert goes on for miles. I could get lost in it and nobody would even know.*

What Lori wanted was to go back to Pickford County and get married and have kids, and never step foot across the county line again.

Chuck

Chuck decided to tell in Phoenix.

He was sick of being sneaky. He was tired of worrying that Lori would tattle on him. His heart pounded and his palms got sweaty every time Mom asked, "So did you two have a good time?"

Just think how awful he'd feel if he were doing something really bad.

Maybe he was. . . .

He pushed the thought away. He'd tell and then everything would be all right. Maybe.

He thought about the artist's pad and colored pencils he'd bought in Philadelphia. He'd seen lots of art students drawing at some of the museums, copying the paintings. Now he'd begun to do that, too, from memory, whenever he could hide from Mom and Lori.

What would it be like not to have to hide anymore?

It was one of those rare nights when Mom wasn't giving a speech. She was sitting at the table in the hotel room, writing notes in the margins of a stack of papers. Lori was sprawled across one of the beds watching TV. Chuck eased into the chair across from Mom.

"Mom," he started, and almost lost his nerve. He reminded himself he was in Phoenix, farther from home than he'd ever been before in his life. He was safe.

Mom looked up, waiting.

"I'm too dumb to be a farmer," Chuck blurted out.

Oh no! Why did I say that?

Chuck braced himself for Mom to say what she'd have to say: *Of course you're not too dumb. You just have to try harder. Listen to Pop. Pay attention in vo-ag class. I have faith in you.* Lies, lies, lies. And Chuck would have to pretend to believe her.

But Mom just gave him a steady look.

"I'm too dumb to be a farmer, too," she said.

Chuck's mouth was already forming the obedient, meaningless, *Okay, Mom. I'll try harder. Whatever you say.* He froze when she said the wrong thing.

"Huh?" he managed to grunt.

"So are most of the people I've met, traveling around," Mom said. "Farmers have to know about everything—botany, animal science, mechanical engineering, commodity trading, international markets. . . . Then there's all the physical labor. There aren't many people in this country anymore who'd last even a month or two on a farm. Pop

114

may give you all that 'I'm just a dumb old farmer' spiel, but don't believe it. He's a genius in coveralls."

Chuck stared at Mom, his mouth hanging open. Fine. Pop was a genius. How was that supposed to make Chuck feel better?

"But I'm dumb," he repeated.

"You—," Mom started and hesitated.

Chuck was suddenly too mad to listen. His own mother wouldn't even deny it. He was dumb.

"The other kids tease me," he said. "You know that, don't you?"

"Chuck, you just have to know how to deal with them," Lori said from across the room. "Just get along."

Chuck turned on her.

"'Just get along'? How am I supposed to do that? Laugh along with them when they call me Chuck *Lard*son? Hold my tests up so everyone can look at the big fat F's at the top? Stand up at the front of the room during vo-ag so everyone sees I can't put a tractor engine back together?"

Chuck was breathing hard, winded just from talking. Why couldn't he shut up? All he'd meant to do was announce, *I've been going to art museums.* Where had all that other stuff come from? Now Mom would know what he was really like. Chuck's face flamed. Images tumbled through his mind. Phys ed class with half the reserve football team, all of them pointing and laughing while footballs slipped through Chuck's arms. English papers handed back with big red circles and nasty comments written above every other word. FFA meetings where everyone else sat together, and Chuck sat alone in a row of empty chairs. Pop's face, red and angry, his mouth open, yelling something: "How many times do I have to tell you to shut the gate? . . . What in the world were you thinking, driving a tractor like that? . . . You trying to kill that corn, spraying anhydrous like that?"

"Oh, Chuck," Mom said, so softly it sounded like an echo. Maybe it was an echo. In his mind, Chuck saw the face of another woman who had spoken his name like that. Miss Prentiss, his first-grade teacher.

"Oh, Chuck, you are not stupid," she'd say. "Don't you pay any attention to what those other kids say. Different people just learn different ways. Now, you try that top line again. . . ."

Miss Prentiss kept having conferences with Mom and Dad. Chuck sat there squirming while Lori played with dolls and Mikey and Joey toddled around the room.

"Don't you think this is your fault, Chuck," Miss Prentiss would say. "If anyone's stupid, it's us teachers, because we can't figure out how to help you."

After every single one of those conferences, Daddy took Chuck out for ice cream—just Chuck. All the other kids had to go home with Mom.

"I don't think there's anything to worry about, Chuckeroo," Daddy would say. "At least, nothing that a little ice cream won't help. Here. This'll make everything better."

Chuck could still see those cones Daddy gave him, trailing sprinkles and fudge sauce and chopped nuts. They seemed to tower higher than Chuck's head.

Halfway through the school year, Miss Prentiss had gotten some sort of grant and gone off to learn how to help kids read better.

Every teacher Chuck had had since then was sure it was Chuck who was stupid.

And after Daddy died, Chuck had to eat his "make everything better" ice cream alone.

Chuck ate a lot of ice cream. Then he moved on to heaps of meat loaf, mounds of mashed potatoes, bushels of beans, dozens of doughnuts. . . . No matter how much he ate, it was never enough to make everything better.

Sometimes Chuck was almost glad Daddy was dead and Mom was away most of the time, because that meant neither one of them had to know how stupid he was. How worthless.

So what was he doing now, telling Mom?

"Chuck—," Mom tried again. Her voice sounded wobbly. Chuck thought about how she stood in front of thousands of people every night, without getting nervous at all. But *he* was so pathetic, she couldn't get even two words out, talking to him.

Lori came over and leaned against the wall behind Mom.

"It's true," she said matter-of-factly. "People make fun of him a lot. But Chuck's not really *that* stupid. Lots of kids at school are even dumber. Even a lot of the ones who tease him all the time."

Chuck couldn't believe his ears. Was *Lori* defending him? But she wasn't done.

"Chuck's just different," Lori continued. "You know. Chuck doesn't talk about cars or hunting or girls or tractors. He doesn't know a gasket from a gearshift. He likes art. He's been sneaking out to art museums this whole trip. And drawing. He's really good. Want to see?"

Nobody answered, but Lori walked over to Chuck's suitcase, anyway, and pulled out his secret notebook. Chuck's jaw dropped. How had she known? Lori flipped the notebook open and laid it on the table in front of Mom, like some lawyer on TV, presenting evidence to the judge.

Chuck felt naked. What else did she know?

"May I look?" Mom asked.

At least she asked.

Chuck managed to nod. Mom began flipping pages. There was the copy he'd made of the van Gogh painting, where he hadn't gotten any of the perspective right. There was the Rembrandt portrait, where he'd had to erase the nose fifty times, and still hadn't gotten it right. There was the drawing he'd made of Mom speaking. He'd done a great job drawing the podium, but she was flat and lifeless, with none of the sparkle she carried in real life.

"Stop!" Chuck yelled. He yanked the notebook out of Mom's grasp. Clutching it with both hands, he started to pull in opposite directions. He'd rip his pictures into shreds. He wasn't an artist. He never would be.

"No!" Lori and Mom shouted together. Chuck was so surprised to hear them agree on anything that he hesitated. Mom slipped the notebook out of his hands and held it shut on her lap.

Chuck couldn't look at Mom or Lori. Everyone was so quiet, the air conditioner's hum sounded like a roar.

"You don't have to show these to me," Mom said softly. "Or anyone. You have a right to privacy."

"I—," Lori started to protest. Chuck lifted his head in time to see Mom silence her with a look.

"But don't destroy them," Mom said. "They are good."

"You're just saying that," Chuck said sulkily. "I can't do anything right."

It was true. He couldn't divide quadratic equations to save his life. He couldn't dissect a frog without ripping all the vital organs. He couldn't plow a single row without getting distracted and going crooked. He couldn't keep a baby pig from squirming long enough to give it a rhinitis shot. And it was like Lori said: He didn't know a gearshift from a gasket. He didn't care. None of those things mattered to him.

But drawing did. Why couldn't he be good at that?

"Chuck," Mom said gently. "You haven't had any training. Pickford High School doesn't have any art classes, does it?"

Chuck shook his head.

"Then we'll find someone to give you private lessons," Mom promised. "Just don't give up on yourself. Ever. About anything. Okay?"

Chuck found himself nodding. And nodding.

Mom handed him back his notebook.

"Lori, you stay out of Chuck's suitcase. You hear?"

Chuck hugged his notebook to his chest, tighter and tighter.

It was still dark when Lori awoke the next morning. Mom was up already, tiptoeing around. Lori watched through half-closed eyes as Mom pulled on sweats and tennis shoes and slipped out the door.

She's running away from home, Lori thought drowsily. *Nah. She already did that.*

Lori closed her eyes. It was easier to go back to sleep than to think about Mom or Chuck or anything that had happened in the past week and a half.

The next time Lori woke up, sunlight was streaming in the window, and she could hear the shower running in the bathroom. Chuck's bed was empty. The door opened and it was Mom back again, flushed and sweaty.

Lori propped herself up on her elbows.

"Where were you?" she asked sleepily.

"I went jogging," Mom said.

"I didn't know you did that," Lori said.

"I do it a lot, when I'm traveling," Mom said. "It helps me think." She sat down on the edge of Lori's bed. Lori was still close enough to dreaming that she could let herself enjoy having Mom nearby. Maybe Mom was getting ready to tell her more. Lori remembered one time at home when they'd all been in the living room together, and some report had come on TV about people jogging.

"Now, that's a waste of time," Pop had said. "If those folks want to get some exercise, why don't they try doing some honest work for a change?"

And Mom had sat there and not said a word. Lori felt like assuring Mom now, *Don't worry. Your secret's safe with me. I won't tell Pop you jog.* Then maybe she and Mom could laugh about how Pop always made those grand pronouncements that didn't really mean a thing. All bark, no bite, that was Pop.

Mom glanced toward the bathroom, where the spray of the shower was still pounding away. She leaned in toward Lori. Lori braced herself to receive another secret.

"While it's just you and me," Mom began.

"Yes?" Lori said. Without even thinking about it, she started holding her breath.

"You can tell me. How bad is it for Chuck?" Mom asked.

Chuck. Lori exhaled so hard, she practically snorted.

"What do you mean?" she asked.

"The teasing," Mom said. "Are the other kids really mean?"

"I don't know," Lori said. "I'm not with him twenty-four hours a day."

"You're around him more than I am," Mom said.

It was the perfect opportunity for Lori to spit back, *Whose fault is that?* She managed to keep her mouth shut.

"What do kids say?" Mom asked. "They don't get . . . physically abusive, do they?"

Lori thought about some of the rumors she'd heard. A couple of guys from school had supposedly circled around Chuck at the fair last year, hit him with hog switches, and yelled out, "Piggy! Piggy!" Would Mom call that physically abusive? It was just a harmless prank.

Wasn't it?

"I don't know, Mom," Lori said again. "They call him dumb and stupid and fatso and retard and, I don't know, stuff like that. But it's not like people are beating him up every day or anything."

"But why Chuck?" Mom asked.

Either Mom was still sweating, or there were tears in her eyes. Was Mom crying for Chuck?

Why did that make Lori feel jealous?

"Come on, Mom," Lori said, more harshly than she meant to. "Don't you remember high school at all? Kids make fun of other kids. That's just what they do. Even if you're popular, you've always got to watch out that something doesn't happen to make you seem weird or unpopular or whatever. Like, you know how you want to have

Chuck take art lessons? That's not going to help. Nobody takes art lessons. It'll just make him seem weirder than ever."

"But Chuck wants art lessons," Mom said. "I'm sure of it."

Had Mom ever asked Lori what she wanted?

"Maybe," Lori said. "But, see, this is how it works. Something like that could even make *me* look bad—"

Lori had said the wrong thing again. She knew it as soon as the words were out of her mouth. Mom drew back, looking horrified.

"Oh, sorry," she snapped. "I forgot that your image was more important than Chuck."

"No, Mom, listen—," Lori scrambled to explain. She couldn't stand to have Mom looking at her that way again. How had this happened? How come Lori knew what to say to everyone except her own mother?" I mean, I don't really care if he takes art lessons or not. I mean, I guess it'd be good for him. And, really, if his being weird was going to hurt my image, that would have happened a long time ago—"

"I think you've said quite enough," Mom said.

"No, wait," Lori pleaded. She thought about all the times on this trip that Mom had given her that appalled look. Until now, Lori knew she had deserved every single one of them. She deserved it on that first airplane trip, when Chuck threw up, and Lori was mean, and Mom sliced her into shreds with a single glance. Lori deserved the looks in Chicago, when she kept asking nasty questions, and Mom's answers got icier and icier and icier, until Lori was sure she finally understood the meaning of "absolute zero."

But Lori hadn't deserved Mom's glares last night or the cruel way she'd snapped, "You stay out of Chuck's suitcase. You hear?" And she didn't deserve Mom's anger now. Lori had been trying to help Chuck, showing Mom his drawings. She'd been, well, almost proud of him, wanting someone else to see what he could do. It wasn't even like she'd been snooping in his suitcase to begin with. She'd just seen his drawing pad hidden under his bed back in Philadelphia, and she'd picked it up, thinking some other guest had left it behind.

But had Mom given her a chance to explain that?

And this morning, she was just trying to get Mom to understand what it was like for Chuck at school. And for Lori. It wasn't Lori's fault other kids were mean.

Or was it?

Lori thought about all the times she'd heard other kids call to Chuck, "Hey, Lardson," all the times she'd heard them taunt, "Do you even have a brain?"

Could she have stopped them?

She thought about the postcard she'd almost sent from Atlanta, making fun of Chuck for sneaking out to art museums. Did that count as joining in?

"Mom," Lori pleaded again, but it was no use. She sounded guilty now. She was guilty.

Chuck came out of the bathroom just then, and Mom

and Lori sprang apart instantly, like they were doing something wrong. Like they had to hide the fact that they'd been talking about him. Chuck looked dazedly from Mom to Lori.

Lori stared back at Chuck like he was some stranger she'd never seen before. Like he was an exhibit in a museum.

He was fat. But he wasn't really any fatter than lots of other kids back home—Robert Hayes, for example, who was some big star on the football team. Nobody teased Robert.

Chuck had his mouth open slightly, and that made him look dumb. But he had to breathe through his mouth sometimes because he had bad allergies. It wasn't his fault.

Chuck was wearing stiff new blue jeans and a polo shirt Mom had gotten him, with vertical red-and-blue stripes. (Had Mom thought that would be slimming?) The shirt was a little too big on him, and maybe too grown-up. It looked like he'd borrowed it from some businessman at a conference Mom had spoken at—like one of them had said, *I brought this because I thought I was going to have time to play golf, but I didn't. Want it for your son?* Chuck just didn't look comfortable wearing that shirt.

Did Chuck *ever* look comfortable?

Chuck still had comb marks in his wet hair, and that made him look younger. For just a second, Lori saw past the fat and the dumb expression and the ill-fitting shirt. She saw the little boy who had been her best friend and constant companion. The one she would have walked barefoot across a field of burrs and thistles for. The one she worried about when he got carsick. ("Chuckie okay now? Chuckie okay now?" she used to ask, again and again, because her whole world depended on hearing the right answer.)

The one she'd been mad at for the past eight years, without even knowing why.

Lori waited for the familiar fury to hit her again, but it didn't come right away.

"Chuck," she said weakly. "When we get home and you start taking art lessons, if anyone makes fun of you for it, I'll make them stop."

At the same time, Mom was saying, "Chuck, we need to figure out how to deal with those kids who are making fun of you. Who are they? I bet I went to school with the parents of pretty much everyone in your class. If you tell me who's teasing you, I could make some calls, talk to their parents—"

Lori had wanted Mom to notice what Lori was saying. She turned on Mom.

"Mom, that's crazy. You can't call people's parents. That will just make everyone tease him more," she said.

"Well, we've got to do something. What those kids are doing—that's harassment. No one should have to put up with that." She glared at Lori. "Do you have any better ideas? Anything you could do that won't hurt your *image*?"

Lori looked back at Chuck. His eyes were darting back and forth—toward Lori, toward Mom, toward Lori, toward Mom. He reminded Lori of a caged animal looking for an escape.

Chuck had had a nightmare.

It started out happy. He dreamed that he and Mom and Dad were having a conference with Miss Prentiss, his first-grade teacher, and she had said, "Oh, forget about reading and math. They don't really matter, not when he's so talented otherwise. Have you seen how Chuck can draw?"

Daddy had clapped him on the back and said, "Way to go, son." They'd gone out for ice cream to celebrate, not to make up for everything Chuck couldn't do.

But while Chuck was sitting there digging into mounds of Dairy Queen soft serve, Daddy had disappeared. Poof. Now you see him, now you don't. Chuck got up from his little stone table and walked all around the Dairy Queen parking lot yelling, "Daddy! Daddy! Where are you?" And people were laughing at him. All the kids he knew were high school students, pointing and snickering and calling out, "Dummy! Fatso!" But Chuck was still a little boy who couldn't see over the pick-up truck beds. The cars and trucks were parked like a maze, and Chuck couldn't find his way out.

Then he ran smack into Miss Prentiss, between a red Ford and a blue Chevy. She was shaking her head sadly.

"Oh, Chuck," she sighed. "You know why this happened."

She kept shaking her head, but she stopped being Miss Prentiss. She turned into Mrs. Swain, his second-grade teacher. Then she turned into Mom.

Chuck woke up soaked in panicky sweat. His heart was racing, and he couldn't catch his breath. He got up and stumbled into the bathroom, turned on the shower full blast. He climbed in shakily and stood there letting the stream of water beat against his skin. It cleared away the sweat but did nothing for the jumble in his mind.

Had the dream Miss Prentiss/Mrs. Swain/Mom said, "You know why this happened," or "You know what will happen now"?

Chuck stayed in the shower long past the point that Pop would have been yelling, back home, "You gonna leave any water for the rest of us?" These fancy hotels always had lots of water pressure. He kept thinking the shower would wash away everything. But this was as useless as pressure-spraying the hog barn. Some things could never be washed away.

The whole bathroom was filled with steam when he

finally turned off the water and pulled back the curtain. Now it was silence that roared in his ears. No, not silence—he could still hear the words from his dream. They were definitely, "You know what will happen now."

A warning.

Chuck stepped out and toweled off; his hands shook as he pulled on his clothes. He pushed open the door just to get away from the fog, but it trailed after him.

Mom and Lori were sitting on the bed together. They both jumped when they saw him.

"Chuck," Lori said.

"Chuck," Mom said.

They were both talking at once. Chuck didn't catch a single word either of them said. Wait. Did Lori say, "art lessons"?

Chuck had almost forgotten. He'd agreed to take art lessons. Art lessons meant he'd keep drawing once they got back to Pickford County.

He couldn't.

He looked from Mom to Lori and back again. He was too stricken to make sense of what they were saying, but their voices pushed at him, picked at him, pressured him. Lori's words still pounded in his ears. "Art lessons . . . Art lessons . . ."

Panic sent Chuck halfway across the room.

"Forget it!" he yelled. "I don't want art lessons. Ever!"

He jerked his artist's notebook out of his suitcase. He threw back the cardboard covers and grasped the inside pages, everything he'd drawn. In one motion, he'd ripped all his drawings in half.

"See?" he said, panting like a dog. "I hate art. I won't be different anymore."

Mom and Lori stared back at him, their eyes huge. Maybe one of them said something. Chuck didn't hear. He was noticing how much Mom and Lori looked alike, how they tilted their heads the same, raised their eyebrows the same. Why couldn't they get along? They were so much alike—Lori was the queen of Pickford County, and Mom had the whole country applauding her every night. If he ever drew a picture of the two of them together like this, maybe they'd see—

No. He'd already forgotten: He'd never draw another picture.

Lori

Los Angeles.

This was the only place on the whole itinerary Lori had wanted to go. Before the trip, she'd lain in bed imagining talking about it afterward: *Oh, yes, when I was in Los Angeles . . .* On the first day of school, maybe. Kids would turn around in the hall and shoot her looks of amazement and envy.

It would be obnoxious, she knew. She'd have to be careful not to drop "Los Angeles" into too many conversations, or people would hate her for it. But Los Angeles was the pinnacle of cool, the home of hip, the seat of scandal—it stood for everything that Pickford County wasn't. Lori just wanted a little bit of that reflected glory to rub off on her. Sometimes she worried that the guys back home thought she was too staid, as if she came with her own apron attached, a housewife already. Sometimes she felt like their own mothers, when she was leading 4-H meetings: "And the next item of business is—Jason, would you please get your feet off that table? You're getting mud everywhere." No wonder she'd never had a serious boyfriend, the way all of her friends had.

She'd thought that if she'd been to L.A., maybe the guys would see her through an aura of starlet glamour. Sexiness by association.

But now, watching out the window as their plane prepared to land, she couldn't summon up so much as a shred of eagerness, even when she thought she glimpsed the huge HOLLYWOOD sign through the clouds. This whole trip had been such a disaster, all she wanted was to go home. Even if it meant being seen as staid forever, she just wanted Mom to deposit her and Chuck back safely with Gram and Pop. Gram and Pop didn't blame Lori for Chuck's problems.

Gram and Pop can't see through me like Mom does. Gram and Pop think I'm a good kid. I can fool them.

Lori pushed such thoughts aside. She *was* a good kid. She'd just forget everything that happened in Phoenix, and everything else Mom had said. Lori didn't owe Chuck anything. As far as Lori was concerned, once she was home again, she didn't care what happened to Chuck. Or Mom. It'd be just fine with Lori if Mom went back out on the road forever, flipping and flapping from coast to coast, traveling as much as that guy they'd read about in English. The Ancient Mariner. Did he ever go home?

Home, Lori thought longingly. *Oh, if only the plane were taking off, instead of landing.*

And then, strangely, just as she thought that, the plane jerked up, its nose pointed back toward the sky.

Chuck

Chuck was not wearing his airsickness bracelets.

Were you trying to make me look different? he wanted to ask Mom. Normal guys didn't wear bracelets. They didn't have to.

I hate my life, Chuck thought. *I hate myself.*

His braceletless wrist twitched against the airplane seat, and he realized he'd begun to trace a design on the weave of the fabric.

Stop that, he commanded himself. He wasn't allowed to draw, ever again.

Suddenly the plane practically hopped in the air, turning strangely.

Maybe it's going to crash, Chuck thought, almost hopefully. He hoped Lori and Mom got out safely. And the other people. He didn't want anyone to die.

Except himself.

Lori

The plane's P.A. system crackled.

"The control tower has informed us we need to circle the airport another time before landing," the pilot said. "Due to the weather system coming in, they've closed a runway and the jets are stacking up."

The clouds outside the window were ominous and gray. Lori had flown—what? five times now?—and she'd never thought before about any of her planes crashing. Why not? Had she thought no plane would dare crash with Lori Lawson on board?

Lori groaned silently. She was worried now. It was just too weird, the way the plane was jerking around. Like the plane was fighting the wind, and losing.

"We'll likely be experiencing some turbulence during the landing," the pilot continued. "Please obey the 'fasten seat belts' sign."

Lori looked over at Mom.

"Is this safe?" she asked.

"They wouldn't land if it weren't," Mom said. "Don't worry. I've landed in lots worse weather. Think of it as, I don't know, a wild roller coaster ride."

But roller-coaster cars were on wheels, strapped to rails, held up by crisscrosses of solid steel bars hammered into the ground. This plane was in the middle of the sky. Nothing was holding it up.

Nothing. Not steel, not wheels, not God. Just—what was it that kept planes up, anyway? Air?

"Flight attendants, prepare for landing," the pilot said tensely.

Lori had to have something solid to hang on to. She clutched the armrests.

"Would they tell us?" she asked Mom. "If the plane was going to crash, would they let us know?"

Mom's eyes were on the telephone built into the seat in front of her.

"No," she admitted. "Probably not. But we're not going to crash."

Lori wanted to ask if Mom was just considering calling the convention organizers, to let them know that her flight was delayed. Or did she want to call home to talk to Gram and the other kids one last time?

If the plane was going to crash, Lori wondered, *would Mom tell us?*

No. Probably not.

The plane began to shake violently. The noise was terrible. Lori thought about tornadoes, hurricanes, typhoons. The plane dived into darker clouds. Rain lashed against the window.

Oh, no . . . , Lori thought, and it was like something that Mom said in just about all her speeches. Mom hid it with jokes and wordplay, but really all she ever talked about was dying—dying without thinking, *Oh no, I always meant to . . .*

God? Lori whispered silently. *I have way too many "Oh no"s to die now.*

Probably everyone on the plane felt that way.

Probably Daddy had felt that way, too, eight years ago. He probably wanted to live long enough to see Emma born. He probably wanted to see all his kids grow up. He probably wanted to farm for another fifty years. He probably wanted to be able to retire someday and travel around the country with Mom.

And Mom—

Lori turned toward her mother. If the plane was going to crash, the very least she could do was say something to Mom. Something real. Something she meant, not something hidden in sarcasm or nastiness or fake charm. And then probably she should apologize to Chuck. Lori had about eight years' worth of apologies to make to both of them, Mom and Chuck, before the plane hit the ground.

Lori had her mouth open, the words gathering in her mind, before she saw what Mom and Chuck were doing.

Chuck was throwing up into his airsickness bag. And Mom was patting his back, practically cooing, "It's all right. You're okay."

Didn't Mom have any regrets? Wasn't there even one *Oh no* pealing in her mind?

Didn't she have anything she wanted to say to Lori?

Chuck

This was all he deserved: the queasy stomach, the instant gag reflex, the plane shivering around him.

Then they were on the ground, gliding toward the gate. They weren't going to crash.

Was Chuck disappointed or relieved?

Mom still had her hand on his back. Just that light touch made it impossible for him to decide.

Around them, people were reaching for their carry-on bags, taking off their seat belts, grumbling about the rough landing. They were like statues brought to life. Lori and Chuck and Mom were the only ones not moving.

"We all oughta sue," someone griped behind Chuck.

"Aw, that was nothing," someone else countered. "I used to fly military jets. Our motto was, 'Any landing you survive is a good one.'"

Did I survive? Chuck wondered. "Survive" was such a

funny word. He'd been listed in the newspaper all those years ago as Daddy's survivor. Chuck could remember Gram explaining it to him: "That just means you lived longer than your daddy did." Chuck hadn't been able to understand—his father had been twenty-eight, Chuck was only seven. Twenty-eight was a bigger number than seven. *No, Daddy outsurvived me,* Chuck had wanted to tell Gram and all those other grown-ups.

But there were things you couldn't tell grown-ups. Couldn't ask them, either, because then they looked at you with crinkly worry lines around their eyes.

Chuck hadn't survived. Chuck wasn't surviving.

Mom removed her hand from his back.

"Are you all right?" she asked.

Chuck couldn't answer.

Lori

Another speech.

Lori didn't know how Mom stood it, just about every night, sitting through boring before-dinner introductions, stupid chitchat over rubbery chicken and undercooked broccoli, unfunny jokes about people she didn't even know. And then she had to give the speech itself. Lori wasn't sure what the speech was tonight, but if she had to hear Mom say, "Oh no, I was going to spend more time with my family!" one more time, Lori was going to need an airsickness bag, too.

Of course, hearing Mom say that even once was enough to make Lori puke. But she was trying not to think about anything Mom said. She didn't want Los Angeles to be another Chicago, another Phoenix. She wasn't going to let Mom get to her.

Not after they'd been on that plane, almost crashing,

and Mom hadn't bothered even to say, *I love you* to Lori or Chuck.

The introducer stood up, and Lori braced herself for another maddening burst of praise for Mom, some clump of overblown words that made her sound like someone Lori had never met. This introducer was a tall, thin, Hispanic man (Latino? Chicano? Lori would feel a lot more comfortable about different people if she knew what they wanted to be called.) He seemed supremely confident, waiting calmly at the podium until the banquet room was quiet.

"We have a special speaker for you tonight," the man said.

Oh no. Here we go again, Lori thought.

"I could give you a long list of her awards and accomplishments, but I thought I'd do something a little different," the man continued. "I have a friend at C-SPAN who was able to get me this footage. Watch."

The lights instantly dimmed. A giant blue screen lowered from the ceiling. In seconds, the blue faded, and there, larger than life, was Mom, sitting at a table, leaning toward a microphone. Lori tried to identify the occasion, but it was hard, because what else had Mom done the past eight years but lean into microphones? This must have been fairly early on, because Mom looked a lot younger. Her hair was long and feathered back from her face, the way Lori remembered her wearing it years ago, when Lori was a little girl.

When Dad was still alive.

A flickering label appeared beneath Mom's face: CONGRESSIONAL TESTIMONY, JOAN LAWSON—WIDOW OF INSURED.

Oh, Lori thought. *Oh no.*

Though she couldn't remember anyone ever telling her so, she knew that Mom's whole speaking career was launched because she testified before Congress about Dad's death. Some people saw her on the evening news and were impressed. They invited her to speak at churches and Farm Bureau meetings in surrounding counties. And the next thing anyone knew, she was jetting across the country talking every night.

Lori had never seen her mother's testimony.

On the screen, Mom was biting her lip.

"Yes," she answered some unseen questioner. "My husband and I owned a six-hundred-acre farm in Ohio. That is, we owned what we didn't owe the bank for."

The camera panned back. Some of the congressmen were snickering.

"And then your husband was killed on your farm last fall?" someone asked, his voice dripping with that false sympathy that always made Lori angry.

On screen, Mom didn't even recoil.

"Yes," she said quietly. "The electrical system on one of our tractors malfunctioned. There was a spark. . . . The fuel tank exploded."

"And your husband was on the tractor when this happened?"

"Yes," Mom said.

There was a brief silence. Even congressmen were at a loss for words after that.

Then one of them said, "And your husband went to his grave believing he was well insured?"

Mom hesitated, almost as if she wanted to protest the wording of the question.

"When we had our first child, we bought a life insurance policy that was supposed to provide for our children if anything happened to either of us. We wanted . . . we wanted them to have good lives."

"You're referring to policy number XG1065387, held with the Rylen Insurance Company?"

"Yes," Mom said.

"And you had paid all the premiums on this policy?"

"Yes," Mom said. She took a sip of the water in front of her. "It wasn't cheap. And those were scary times for farmers—two of our neighbors were going through bankruptcies. Several times we talked about taking our chances, canceling the policy and just praying that nothing went wrong. But we knew we could never forgive ourselves if—" She took another drink. Her eyes were misty. Lori thought she looked like one of those people you saw on the evening news all the time, labeled HURRICANE SURVIVOR, TORNADO SURVIVOR, MASSACRE SURVIVOR. She looked practically otherworldly, as if she'd witnessed things nobody else would understand.

The congressmen were waiting for her to finish her sentence, but she didn't. Finally one of them spoke.

"So you had every reason to believe that, upon your husband's death, the Rylen Insurance Company would pay in full?"

Mom nodded.

"But they denied your claim?"

Mom nodded again.

Was that *what Mom's testimony had been about?* Lori wondered. She had never known. Mom had never told her. Gram and Pop had never told her. When she was six years old, her father's death alone seemed like a big enough event that Congress needed to be informed. And after that, nobody talked about it.

Had the insurance company cheated them? Were they poor after Daddy died?

Of course they'd been poor. They'd had to sell their house and farm and move in with Gram and Pop. But Mom had just said, "Won't it be nicer this way? You can see Gram and Pop all the time."

Lori's mind was reeling. She missed some of what Mom and the congressmen were saying, up on the screen. When she started paying attention again, a congressman was saying, "So you were left with nothing?"

"Just—" Mom seemed to be having trouble speaking. "Social security."

"Mrs. Lawson," one of the congressmen asked gently. "You have several children, don't you?"

Mom nodded. But instead of giving a number, she started listing their names.

"There's Chuck," she began slowly. "He's seven. Then there's Lori, who's six." She stretched out their names, as if caressing them. "And Mike, who's three. And Joey, who's two. And Emma, the baby."

It was agony listening to that slow litany of names. Even Lori, who certainly knew how many brothers and sisters she had, felt like the list was endless. Twice, a congressman started to interrupt, as if expecting Mom to be done.

"That's five, right?" a congressman asked when she finally stopped.

"Yes," Mom said. "I have five children."

"And now you have to raise them alone, without the insurance money you had every reason to believe was yours," another congressman said. "Mrs. Lawson, how do you intend to survive?"

Mom's cheeks were flushed. She sat up very straight.

"By the grace of God," she said, "we'll get by."

She sounded almost noble, saying that. All of the congressmen were silenced. Lori got chills, and the banquet hall was so quiet that Lori could hear Chuck breathing behind her. It was that line. Lori felt like she had been watching the scene in *Gone with the Wind* where Scarlett O'Hara raises a fistful of dirt to the sky and proclaims, "I'll never be hungry again." But that was just an actress, pretending, and this was Mom, Lori's mom, for real. Lori had never seen anything so real before in her entire life.

The screen went blank. Beneath it, the flesh-and-blood Mom was walking toward the podium. She seemed to have an incredible distance to go. Lori had a sudden flash of pity for her mother, having to speak now, with the banquet hall still hushed with awe, the image from eight years ago still burning in everyone's minds.

Mom reached the podium and stepped up on a stool. She expertly bent the microphone down to her level.

"Well," she said briskly. "I wish someone had told me then how out-of-date that hairstyle would look now."

Everyone burst out laughing. Lori could almost feel the tension being released. It reminded her of a time last year when she'd gotten a ride home from school with some neighbor kids, and the driver had decided to race the train at the railroad crossing on Ford's Pike Road. The train missed the back bumper of the car by inches—Lori could see the engineer's outraged, worried face close-up. Speeding on down the road, the whole carload had broken out into the same kind of laughter that rolled through the banquet hall now. It wasn't so much that people were amused; it was more that they desperately needed to do something with the air in their lungs.

Everyone seemed so relieved to be laughing that they went on for several minutes. Mom had to hold up her hand for silence.

"That film clip was from a very long time ago," she said. "What I wanted to speak about tonight was the time we can still do something about. The present."

And then Mom rolled into a speech Lori had heard before, in Philadelphia, maybe, or Atlanta. Lori studied her mother without hearing a single one of her words. Mom said something funny and grinned proudly as the crowd laughed again, this time with true mirth.

How can she? Lori wondered. *How can she go on like usual after they showed that film? How can she smile at all?*

Lori herself wanted to cry. No—she wanted to scream. No—she didn't know what she wanted. It was so unfair, the way everything had happened. Daddy shouldn't have died. Mom and Gram and Pop shouldn't have pretended everything was okay. And—maybe—they shouldn't have had to sell their house and farm. Was that true?

Lori felt like there was a blender going full speed inside her, mixing up all her thoughts and emotions. She forced herself to sit up very straight and pretend she was listening to her mother. But she didn't want to sit still, not now. And there was no way she could have heard a single word her mother said over the roaring in her ears.

Chuck listened to the entire videotape of his mother's congressional testimony with his mouth hanging open, in awe.

Mom has really suffered, he thought. *She knows about pain. She understands.*

It was strange how happy that thought made him.

Mom

WHAT JOAN LAWSON WANTED TO SAY
DURING HER SPEECH IN LOS ANGELES:

How dare you. Did you all enjoy that, watching my grief? Was I entertaining enough?

You're all too close to Hollywood. Everything's entertainment here. Did any of you think about the fact that I wasn't acting up there? That my husband really died and I was fighting real tears? That I've got two kids out in the audience who might not be ready to see that yet?

I don't know when I thought Lori and Chuck would be ready to see that particular videotape. Maybe never. I've never watched it myself. I've never wanted to.

Living it was hard enough.

And now you think I'm going to smile and walk to the podium and act like everything's fine—you paid me enough, you deserve to get your jollies from my grief?

I'm smiling. I'm walking to the podium. I'm making a joke. I'm doing what I'm supposed to. I learned a long time ago that you can't crumble to the floor in agony just because you want to.

But don't think you could ever pay me enough for my grief.

WHAT JOAN LAWSON ACTUALLY SAID
DURING HER SPEECH IN LOS ANGELES:

But when the time comes that you're signing that final contract, that's not the moment to think, *Oh no, what am I agreeing to here? Did I read all the fine print?* In life, too, as in law, you've got to pay attention as you go along. You can't rush through, eager to get to the next page, because you might miss a cogent point. You might miss the scent of roses, your two-year-old's best smile, the sound of the high school band marching in the Fourth of July parade. . . . And when you get to the last line of this contract called life—a contract between you and God, if you will—you can't hesitate. You have to grasp the pen firmly and write your last signature with a flourish. Because at the end, there are no more appeals courts, no more addenda, no more codicils. When you've signed your last, you have to put away the documents and go out into the sunshine, knowing you've done your best.

It was all Lori could do not to slam the hotel door.

Mom and Chuck had walked into the room ahead of her. Chuck was sitting on the bed already, untying his shoes. Mom was hanging up the jacket from her suit.

Lori stood with her back against the door, stunned.

Mom started washing off her makeup at the sink.

"That's it?" Lori finally burst out. "Aren't you going to say anything?"

Mom turned her head, her mascara smeared across her face as though she'd been crying.

"What do you want me to say?" she asked.

"I don't know!" Lori exclaimed. "Something! Anything! How about, 'Well, now at least you know what I told Congress. Too bad you had to find out in front of five hundred strangers.' How about, 'Gee, I really meant to tell you about that insurance policy before now.' How about—"

"I'm sorry," Mom said.

Chuck kept his head down, accepting his mother's words. Lori wasn't satisfied.

"'I'm sorry'?" she repeated. "That's all you have to say?"

"I'm sorry you had to see that," Mom said. "It was totally unnecessary for them to show that."

Her tone was calm, refined. It infuriated Lori.

"'Unnecessary,'" she echoed again. "'Unnecessary.' Sifting flour is unnecessary. Double-stitching hems is unnecessary. Algebra is unnecessary. That film clip was—is—"

"Essential," Chuck finished quietly for her.

Lori stared at her brother in surprise. She wouldn't have guessed he even knew the word "essential." But it was exactly right, exactly the word she'd been searching for.

Mom didn't reply. She went back to scrubbing makeup from her face.

"Why did you bring us on this trip?" Lori whispered.

Her ears were ringing again. Her heart beat in panicky thuds. It was like being back on the plane again, convinced she was seconds away from crashing.

Mom wouldn't look directly at Lori and Chuck. She stared at their reflections in the mirror.

"I wanted you to see—," she began. "I wanted you to know—"

Lori couldn't wait for another deliberate answer. It would just be a half answer, anyway. A mask.

"Oh, I know why you brought us," Lori accused. "You wanted to get us to hate Pickford County. Just like you do."

She could have gone on, said, *You wanted us to hate ourselves, too*. But those words didn't tumble out so easily.

"What do you mean? I don't hate Pickford County!" Mom protested. "It's my home!"

"Oh, yeah? Then why aren't you ever there? Why have you spent this whole trip telling Chuck and me how much better the rest of the world is?" This was safe terrain—safer, anyway, than talking about the videotape. Lori started mimicking her mother, "'Chicago has such great shopping—not like Pickford County. Can't get good shopping like this back home.' 'Let's eat out at this fancy restaurant, because you can't get anything but McDonald's back home.' 'Pickford High School doesn't have an art program, does it? Not like a *real* school.' 'If Lori weren't such a Pickford County hick, she'd know better than to wear that stupid 4-H dress outside of her own house.'" Mom hadn't actually ever said that, but Lori felt as though she had.

"Stop it!" Mom commanded.

But Lori was on a roll.

"You don't have to lie to us. You hate Pickford County so much, why didn't you just move us all out of there with you after"—Lori forced herself to say the words—"after Daddy died?"

Mom was blinking rapidly. She swiped one of the stiff, white hotel washcloths against her eyelids. For a minute, Lori wondered if she was wiping away mascara or tears. Then Lori decided she didn't care.

Mom finally turned around to face Lori.

"I don't hate Pickford County," Mom said slowly. "I'd never leave it. When your daddy died, everyone we knew brought us casseroles, for weeks. A bunch of our neighbors got together and finished harvesting all our corn, without even being asked. The auctioneer who sold our farm wouldn't let me pay him. Thirty people offered to baby-sit Mike and Joey during the funeral. For a long time, I got hugs every time I walked into church. And then—when I stopped needing them—the hugs stopped. People knew. It isn't like that, other places. That's why I could never leave Pickford County."

"But you did!" Lori insisted. Tears were gathering in her eyes, but she tried to ignore them. "You do. You leave it all the time. You leave us. And you want us to leave, too."

"Oh, Lori, don't be so melodramatic," Mom said. "I'm not leaving on purpose. It's just my job. And this trip—I just wanted you to understand there's a whole big world out here, beyond the county line. I don't want you to get married at eighteen, like I did, never knowing there are other choices out there."

"But what if that's what I want?" Lori asked.

"Is it?" Mom asked. Her eyes were dry now. She took a step toward Lori. "Got your future husband all picked out already? Who's it going to be? One of those perfect gentlemen who've been picking on Chuck? Poor guy probably doesn't stand a chance. You get your claws in him, he won't know what hit him. Next thing he knows, he'll have a mortgage and a passel of kids to support, and he'll never be able to come up for air."

Lori gasped.

"Is that how it was with you and Dad?" she almost whimpered.

"No," Mom said, shaking her head violently. "No. It wasn't."

Chuck recognized the look on Mom's face. Shame. Abject, heartbreaking, regret-filled shame. Mom backed away from Lori and slumped onto the bed beside Chuck. She looked at him in surprise, like she'd forgotten he was there, witnessing this. Then she put her arm around his shoulder.

Chuck stiffened at first, thinking, *Fifteen-year-old boys are not supposed to let their mothers hug them.* But it felt so good, he decided he didn't care. He leaned into the hug.

"Your father and I were in love," Mom said. "We wanted to get married. We wanted kids. We were happy." Mom squeezed Chuck's shoulder. She patted the bed on the other side. "Come on, Lori. Sit down and we can talk about all of this. Without screaming. Without either one of us screaming."

Mom held her arm out stiffly, like she was just waiting for Lori to slide into position, into her mother's embrace.

Lori wondered how her mother could possibly think she wanted a hug now—from her.

"But you're happier now," Lori said coldly. "Why shouldn't you be? You get to stay in fancy hotels, and people fawn over you, and you don't have to do any real work, and you eat in restaurants. . . . You just jumped at the chance to get out of changing dirty diapers and washing manure out of coveralls. Let Gram do that. You don't care. The day Daddy died was the happiest day of your life."

Oh no. She'd said it. She'd said what she'd been afraid even to think this whole, long trip.

Mom's face went white. So did Chuck's. Lori forged on. The dam was broken.

"And having a dead husband is just like—something you can talk about, to make people feel sorry for you. You're like those people who sell their stories to the tabloids. What you say isn't worth anything anymore, because you've spent it all. You're just a—a shell. And it's our story you sold out. You made it not real anymore. It's like, on that tape, you were real, I could tell you meant what you said. Or at least I thought I could. Maybe you didn't even mean it then. Maybe you were just acting, like you're always acting now. You get in front of an audience, you're like a robot. Someone pushes your button and you talk." Lori didn't even know what she was saying. "And it's not fair! How do I know if you're ever real with me?"

Suddenly Lori was crying so hard, Chuck could barely understand what she said.

Is this how other families act? he wondered.

Mom buried her face in her hands, like she deserved

the onslaught of words. When Lori's last sentence blurred into sobs, Mom looked up.

"You're right," she murmured. "A lot of what you say is right. Not about me being glad when Tom died. Oh no. But the rest—I do give speeches like a robot. I probably even use a fakey accent, like you said back in Chicago." She grinned, but it was a pained grin. Chuck forgot himself for a minute and wondered, *How would someone draw that—a smile that looks like tears?*

"I've always had rules for myself, though," Mom said. "There were things I would never talk about. Tom dying was one of them."

Mom's arm on Chuck's shoulder was becoming a burden. He wanted to shake it off, go watch TV, listen to this conversation from the other side of the room. Because he could tell Lori was going to fly right back into Mom's face with another accusation.

"You talk about death all the time," Lori complained, sniffling. "Oh, sorry—the final signature on the contract, the twenty-ninth minute of the half-hour speech, the closing out of the time-bank account, the—"

"But have you ever heard me say, *When my husband died . . .?* Have you ever heard me share a single memory of your dad?" Mom interrupted. "Little things, yes, a stray comment here and there, but nothing important. It's like when you wanted the anecdotes about you out of my speeches, Lori. Those memories of Tom are *mine.* They're not for sale."

Mom sounded so fierce, it silenced Lori. Chuck was surprised that it was his mouth that opened, his vocal chords that moved, his voice that spoke.

"But they should be ours, too," he said. "We're not just some convention people who never knew him. He was our daddy."

The word "daddy" came out like he'd said it as a seven-year-old boy. He remembered his dream again, searching and searching for his lost father in the maze of cars and jeering people. Suddenly he wanted to tell Mom about that dream, but it would sound silly. Mom wouldn't see what it really meant.

Chuck looked over at Lori instead and braced himself for her next attack. But she was staring at Chuck in astonishment.

How could I have ever thought Chuck was dumb? she wondered. *He's a genius.* In a whisper, Chuck had done what Lori hadn't been able to do with any of her shouting. He'd explained exactly what was wrong with Mom.

Lori could suddenly see how it was, how Mom had kept everything that mattered about Daddy locked up to keep from turning him into just another dreary line in just another dreary speech. She'd held on to him so tightly, she couldn't even unlock her memories for her own children.

Did Mom know she'd done that?

Lori looked over at Mom, who was recoiling from Chuck's words. Mom's arm slipped down from his back, but Mom didn't seem to notice.

"Oh," she said. And then again, "Oh."

Even Lori managed to keep quiet, waiting for Mom to recover. Lori felt like everything depended on this moment. She couldn't force Mom to tell her anything. But maybe, if she kept still, if she let the seconds tick by, if she held herself together . . .

Finally Mom spoke.

"There is something about your father's death I've never told anyone," Mom said softly. "I will tell the two of you. If you want."

Lori inhaled sharply. Chuck pulled back and stared into his mother's face.

"What?" Lori challenged.

"I saw the whole thing," Mom said.

That isn't the "real" I wanted, Lori wanted to protest.

No! Chuck wanted to scream. *I can't hear this!*

Neither of them said anything.

Mom was staring toward a worn patch on the carpet.

"You two had already gotten on the school bus," she began in a hypnotic voice. "It was October. You know October on the farm—if you spend five seconds admiring the leaves, you feel guilty because you've wasted time you could have spent on harvest. Pop and Tom were working together, helping each other out. Pop was driving the combine, and Tom was supposed to be driving wagons back and forth, between the field and the bins."

Chuck gulped. He and Pop had had that same arrangement the last three harvests, ever since he turned twelve and Pop trusted him to drive the tractor. He could picture Pop's bright green John Deere combine circling the field, knocking down the brown stalks of corn, gobbling them up and shelling the cobs. Then Pop would pull over to the side of the field and unload a waterfall of corn into a wagon. And Dad would pull up, unhitch an empty wagon, and hitch the full one onto his tractor. Were Dad's wagons red or green or dull, rusted brown? Chuck didn't know why it mattered, but it did. He hoped Dad had had a shiny new wagon behind his tractor, ready to haul corn.

How could he think that, when he knew Dad never made it to the field that day?

"I was standing at the kitchen sink washing up breakfast dishes," Mom continued. "We didn't have a dishwasher then. I had to practically double over, because my stomach was so big with Emma. Mike and Joey were playing on the floor behind me. I looked out the kitchen window."

Stop! Lori wanted to scream. The dread she felt was like something physical, pressing down on her. She didn't want to know what was going to happen next. What had happened next.

"Looking out that window, you could practically see the whole farm, remember?" Mom asked wistfully. And Chuck remembered. He could picture it now: a tangled garden, an almost-turned bean field, a red barn with open doors. And Daddy climbing onto a tractor.

"Tom turned the key," Mom said slowly. "And I saw something. A spark."

"You saw the spark?" Lori asked.

"I think," Mom said. "But how could I have? Maybe it

was just a glint of sunlight. Maybe I just had a premonition. I felt like something was wrong. I opened the window, and I was going to yell to Tom, *Get off the tractor!*"

"Did you?" Chuck asked.

Mom shook her head silently, tears collecting in her eyes.

"I heard Mike behind me, screaming, 'Mommy, look! Mommy, look!' And when I turned around, Joey had climbed up on top of the high chair and was standing on the tray. He was about to fall. I grabbed him as quick as I could. It didn't even take a minute. But when I looked back out the window—"

Mom stopped. Silence pooled around the three of them, like something they could drown in.

"Dad's tractor was on fire," Lori finally said, because nobody else would.

Mom nodded.

"I saw it explode," she said. "I didn't hear it, but I saw it—isn't that weird? I saw the flames, all over. It didn't seem real. Or I couldn't make myself understand what I was seeing. I threw Joey down in the playpen, and I went running out the door. All the way there, I kept praying, 'Oh, please, let Tom be alive. Please, God. Please.'" Her voice dropped to a whisper. "And then at a certain point, you realize what you're praying for isn't possible anymore."

Chuck was seeing his father inside a fireball. Orange and red were such awful colors together. Had Daddy known what was happening? Did he know he was going to die?

"Pop was the one who called 911," Lori said accusingly.

"It didn't even occur to me," Mom said. It sounded like she was apologizing. "I was in shock. I went back inside, and Mike and Joey were both crying because I'd left them. I pulled them both onto my lap, and I hugged them, and I said, 'It's okay, it's okay,' over and over again."

"But it wasn't," Lori said. "You were lying."

Mom gave her a long look.

"They were not-quite-two and three. What was I supposed to say?"

Chuck was working everything out in his head.

"You wouldn't have had time to warn Dad," he said. "Even if it hadn't been for Joey on the high chair."

Mom looked at him gratefully. But, "Wouldn't I?" she asked. "I don't know. I've replayed it in my mind a million times, and I can see Tom jumping down, flattening himself against the ground when the fire came. Like in a war movie. Then getting up safe. Unharmed."

"Why didn't Pop know?" Lori asked. "That you saw everything, I mean."

"Because when he came inside to call 911, I was sitting on the couch reading *Good Night, Moon* to Joey and Mike. The tractor was still burning, but I didn't care about that. Everything that mattered was already gone."

"Pop thinks tractors matter a lot, too," Chuck said. He didn't mean it to be funny, but it was.

Nobody laughed.

"I couldn't have explained," Mom said. "And then, everyone kept treating me like I was made of glass. They tiptoed around me and whispered and whisked you kids away from me every chance they got. And all I wanted to do was grab ahold of all of you, and never let go."

She reached for Lori, and this time Lori didn't protest being pulled into a hug. But after just a second, she shrugged Mom's arm off her shoulder and leaned away.

"You act like telling us all this is some big gift," Lori complained. She'd been expecting something like a fairy godmother's special blessing. No—a mother's blessing. That should be even better. Lori had wanted some secret that would protect her forever. What she'd gotten was just more to mix her up. "I don't know what to *do* with what you've told us."

"Neither do I," Mom said.

All three of them stared at the same patch of carpet, swirls upon swirls upon swirls. It was like a maze. Lori tried to follow the pattern with her eyes, but she kept getting lost and having to start over.

That's this whole trip, Lori thought. *We fly all over the country, but just about every conversation we have leads back to the farm, eight years ago, and Daddy dying. And Mommy leaving us, too.*

"Are you going to tell Joey and Mike?" Chuck asked. "About Joey almost falling off the high chair, and Mike yelling, right when you were going to warn Dad?"

"I don't know," Mom said. "Should I? What do you think?"

It made Chuck feel good, the way Mom said that. She wasn't asking, "What do you think?" like teachers did, when they knew the right answer and were just waiting for you to say something wrong. This was more like she didn't have an answer, and she thought maybe Lori and Chuck did.

"You don't want them to feel guilty," Lori said. "Because it wasn't their fault."

"No," Mom agreed. "I wouldn't tell them now, anyway. Maybe when they're older. Like you two."

Lori felt a little glow—*Mom trusts us!* She thought about her rough-and-tumble younger brothers and felt sorry for them. If she were either of them, she would feel responsible, as if she'd caused her father's death. But she didn't blame them. Probably they wouldn't blame themselves, either. They wouldn't even take the blame for leaving the toilet seat up.

Chuck was thinking, *Now Joey and Mike will have something to deal with, too.* He wasn't sure what he meant by that. He could just see his younger brothers, hitting home runs like it was as natural as breathing, easily guiding their 4-H hogs around the ring, begging Pop to drive the tractor instead of running from the chore. They always fit in so well. Everything was so simple for them. But this bombshell was waiting for them somewhere in the future.

For the first time in years, Chuck felt like the big brother, wanting to protect his younger siblings. Maybe

Mom should never tell. Maybe she shouldn't have told him and Lori.

"I've always wondered—was God offering me a choice?" Mom mused aloud. "My husband or my child?"

"Mo-om!" Lori was shocked. "God doesn't work that way. Besides, falling off the high chair wouldn't have killed Joey."

Mom didn't seem to hear her.

"It felt like I made a choice," she said. She looked straight at Lori. "You accused me of being happy that Tom died. You have to know I wasn't. I would have given anything I had—anything I have—to have him back, alive again. Anything except one of you kids."

Lori gulped.

Chuck & Lori

In the morning, they were all extrapolite with one another, like people tiptoeing around an invalid.

"If you'd rather take the first shower, you can," Lori offered Chuck, even though she'd practically trampled his toes to get ahead of him in every other city.

"Will the noise bother you if I turn on *Good Morning, America* to check the weather?" Mom asked Lori.

"Should I start the coffeemaker for you?" Chuck asked Mom. "I can, if you want."

When they were all ready, Mom beckoned Lori and Chuck over to the small, round table at the back of the hotel room, where she was sitting. The tabletop was strewn with maps and guidebooks and tourist brochures, giving Lori quite a jolt.

Los Angeles? We're in Los Angeles? She'd practically forgotten. She pulled a drape back from the window, and a palm tree brushed the other side of the glass. Surreal. It seemed like a mirage.

"Do you want to go to Hollywood or Disneyland today?" Mom asked. "I thought we'd have time to do some planning last night, but . . ." She let the words trail off. Nobody needed to be reminded of what they'd talked about instead.

So that's how it is, Lori thought. *Daddy dying is a taboo subject again.*

"Hollywood's a lot seedier than you would expect," Mom said. "But it's still one of those places you feel like you have to see. If we don't get to it today, we can always swing by tomorrow before the airport. Disney's a full day, of course. I know you guys are too old for Mickey Mouse, but you'd love Space Mountain, Lori. And, Chuck, you might like—"

"Why didn't you sue?" Lori asked.

Mom froze.

"What?" she said.

"Why didn't you sue?" Lori asked again. "The tractor company or the insurance company or somebody. For Daddy dying."

Mom straightened a pile of brochures, as if it really mattered that the corners were lined up.

"You can't do this," she said. "You can't keep ambushing me. That's all over, okay? We can't live in the past. Weren't you listening to my speech last night?" She grinned, as if trying to let Lori know she was half joking.

Lori shook her head stubbornly. *No. I wasn't listening. I had other things on my mind.*

"Could you have sued?" Chuck asked.

Mom looked from her daughter to her son and sighed.

"Okay," she said. She shoved the guidebooks and tourist pamphlets and maps to the floor. Chuck and Lori watched in amazement. Mom didn't seem to care what a mess she'd made. She didn't even look. When the table was clear, Mom folded her hands in front of her. "Let's get this all out now. I talk, you talk, and then we let this go. All right?"

Speechlessly, Chuck and Lori nodded. Mom took a deep breath.

"Suing," she said, "was never an option. Do you know how old that tractor was? It ran on gasoline, not diesel, you know—I'm not sure anyone was still making gasoline tractors when *I* was born. The tractor company had gone out of business years ago. So there was no tractor company to sue."

"Why didn't Daddy have a safer tractor?" Lori asked in a small voice.

Mom gave her a long look.

"Come on, Lori, you've grown up on a farm. You know how things are. You make do, you get along, you gamble that the tractor'll make it just one more year and that the crops will be good enough that you can buy a new one. And then if the crops aren't so hot, or the bottom falls out of the prices, you gamble that the tractor'll make it two more years, if the combine doesn't break down first, in which case that tractor had better make it three more years—"

Mom's just giving a speech again, Lori thought.

But then Mom stopped herself and looked straight at Lori.

"Nobody thought that tractor was unsafe," she said, and now she sounded as if every syllable hurt. Lori could tell she wasn't hiding behind glib words anymore. "What happened was a fluke—a freak accident. The odds against it were a million to one."

In the hall outside their hotel room, a little kid was shouting about beating his daddy to the swimming pool. Lori and Chuck and Mom could hear a man shouting back, "Oh, yeah? Think you're faster than me?" There was the sound of running. Then there was silence.

"Well, the insurance company owed you," Lori insisted.

"They were bankrupt," Chuck said. "Weren't you listening last night?"

Lori looked at her brother in surprise. He could sit through an entire 4-H meeting and come home and not have the slightest idea when the next meeting was or where they were supposed to turn in their registration forms or who had been elected to Junior Fair Board. But he'd understood Mom's testimony, and all that had stuck with Lori was Mom's last line: "By the grace of God, we'll get by."

"I wasn't paying much attention," Lori admitted.

"The company was running a scam," Mom said. "Tom and I should have read the fine print. The head honcho ran off with the money and put the company in bankruptcy. And there were enough loopholes in the law that he pretty much got away with it."

Mom looked over the table edge at the pile of glossy brochures, and Chuck thought, *That's it. She's not going to tell us anything else.* But then Mom sighed and looked back at them.

"Actually," she said, "I could have sued. I had lawyers calling me, telling me I had a million-dollar case. But . . . there was no guarantee. I could have spent years on a lawsuit and gotten nothing. It all felt like a scam again."

"But that's no reason—," Lori started in heatedly.

Mom gave her a wary look, and Lori shut up.

"My husband had died," Mom said. "I had just given birth. It was all I could do to get out of bed in the morning. The only reason I could get out of bed, I think, was because somebody had to feed Emma, and somebody had to change Joey's diapers, and somebody had to keep Mike from sticking forks in electrical outlets, and somebody had to make sure you two had clean clothes to wear to school. . . . I thought that that somebody had to be me. Because if it wasn't, I had no reason to live, either." Mom stopped, like she'd forgotten what she was trying to say and needed to get back on track. "You know what Gram and Pop think about lawyers. Gram and Pop told me I couldn't trust those crooked lawyers any more than I'd been able to trust the insurance salesman. I was glad to let someone else do my thinking for me."

"But—," Lori objected.

Mom shrugged.

"Just last year, I read that some court dismissed the last of the suits against the insurance company. Nobody got anything," Mom said. "So it wouldn't have mattered."

"It wouldn't have brought Daddy back to life," Chuck said softly, and Mom nodded.

Why did Chuck like that so much, having Mom agree with him?

"But you testified before Congress," Lori persisted. "What good did that do?"

"They wanted to change the law, close the loopholes, so no other insurance company could do what ours did," Mom said.

"I bet Gram and Pop didn't want you to talk to Congress, either," Chuck said. He'd heard Pop's opinions about Congress: "Bunch of crooks in bed with thieves— they don't care about real people, you know that? They don't even try to do what's good for us. The only people they listen to are those lobbyists. The ones who can give them trips on their fancy jets, expensive meals with the liquor flowing. . . . It makes me sick."

"No," Mom said, "they didn't. But I was starting to wake up, starting to think for myself. . . . Even if Congress couldn't force the insurance company to pay us,

I thought I had to make sure nothing like that ever happened to anyone else. Or I could never look any of you kids in the face again." She got a distant look in her eyes. "I can remember packing to go to Washington. . . . I felt like I was traveling to the moon, you know? I had to take Emma with me, because I was still nursing, and I couldn't be away from her very long. They promised there'd be someone to take care of her while I was testifying. They put me up in some fancy hotel, and I was like Gomer Pyle, gone to the big city. 'Shazam! People live like this?' But Emma couldn't sleep in the strange crib, so she cried all night, and I didn't get any sleep. I was so tired, I wanted to cry, too. They put me in front of that microphone, with those bright lights on me, and I felt so stupid that I didn't think I could put two words together."

Lori could remember her mother going off to Washington, D.C. "She's going to talk to the president," she'd bragged at school, because nobody in first grade had ever heard of Congress. But Washington scared Lori. She was afraid "Joanie's going to Washington" was just the grown-ups' way of saying that Mom was going to die, too.

Lori stared out the window at a palm frond that still didn't seem real. Was that really what she had feared? Why hadn't she remembered that before?

"But, Mom, you were great," Chuck was saying. "You were . . . awesome."

"Oh, honey, you weren't there. Videotape lies. I didn't manage to say a single thing I wanted to," Mom said, shaking her head ruefully. "And then I got so mad, because that one congressman kept trying to make it seem like a crime that I had five children. He wanted me to say that we were going to have to go on welfare and be a burden to society, and I was determined—even if I made a total fool of myself—that I wasn't going to give him that satisfaction."

"But then you were famous, and people all over the country wanted to hear you speak," Lori said.

"It wasn't like that," Mom said. "I went home like some dog running off with his tail between his legs. I never wanted to leave Pickford County again."

Lori was so surprised, she jerked back and almost tipped over her chair. *Mom* had felt like that?

"Then the Highland County Farm Bureau asked me to speak to them, and I didn't feel like I could say no. You should have seen me working on my speech. It took me two weeks. Hardest thing I've ever done in my life."

Chuck realized he had seen his mother working on her speech. He could remember her sitting at the kitchen table beside him, while he sweated over arithmetic homework. He erased holes in his work paper. Mom snapped her pencil in two.

"I *stuttered* giving that speech," Mom said. "I figured the whole county felt so sorry for me, that had to be the reason the Highland Presbyterian Church Women's Association asked me to speak at their spring luncheon." Mom had a half smile on her face, remembering. "Afterward, they gave me an envelope with a check inside, and I thought it was charity, like they'd taken up an offering for me because we were so poor. I tried to give it back, I was so humiliated, but they kept saying, 'That's your stipend. Your honorarium.' I didn't even know what those words meant. I didn't know people got paid for talking, unless they were preachers."

"But you liked it," Lori said fiercely. "You liked talking more than you liked staying home with us."

Mom looked steadily at her.

"Oh, Lori, I hated it. I felt like such a fool. Every time I got up to speak, I felt like there was a—a brick in the pit of my stomach. And I missed you all so much, it was like being turned inside out every time I had to leave."

"So why'd you do it?" Lori challenged.

"At first, I felt like I owed people something. Like maybe Tom had died for a reason, and the reason was that I had to warn people not to take their husbands and wives and kids for granted. I never expected to make a career of this. I just took every speech as it came. But they kept coming. And people kept handing me checks. I started doing the math. I realized I could make minimum wage flipping burgers at McDonald's, and you all could be kids who got free lunches at school and bought all your clothes from yard sales; or I could go on the road, and you could have piano lessons and dance lessons and pay 4-H club dues and wear the same clothes as everyone else."

Mom's eyes begged Lori and Chuck to say, *You made*

the right decision. We're glad you did what you did. But Chuck was wondering, *How could Mom hate something she was so good at? And if she hated it, how could she bear to keep doing it?* Lori kept her lips pressed tightly together. Mom filled the silence.

"After a while, when I realized I was going to be speaking a lot, I stopped hating it so much. I got better at it. It was kind of fun, like being in a play. I knew my lines. But it was still hard, being away from you kids. Every second I was away, I worried about you—even the times when you would have been in school and I wouldn't have seen you anyway. Then—" Mom hesitated, as if she wasn't sure how much she should say. Lori and Chuck kept quiet, waiting. Mom went on. "One night my flight got delayed. I should have been home before supper, but it was past you kids' bedtime before I pulled into the drive. Gram came out apologizing, right and left: 'They were just so tired. If I'd known when you were getting home, I'd have kept them awake.' I tiptoed into your room, Lori, hoping you were still up and we could talk, and you could tell me about which of your friends wasn't speaking to which of your other friends. But you were already sound asleep. You looked so peaceful, with your hair spread out on your pillow, that I realized you didn't really need me. Gram was giving you everything you needed. After that, I didn't worry so much. It was like you had given me permission to be away."

Lori was blinking fast, to ward off tears.

"I remember that night," Lori said. "But I was only

faking. I wasn't really asleep. I was . . . being mean."

"Really?" Mom said.

"But it's okay," Lori said. "It was okay."

It's kind of like I did give her permission, by deciding not to care, Lori thought. *How strange—that Mom and I let go at the same time. And neither one of us knew it.*

Lori reached out her hand, and Mom clasped it in hers. Both of them were crying. Maybe they hadn't let go at all. They were linked together again, tight as a chain fence. They looked across the table, and there was Chuck, sitting alone. The outsider again. Mom reached her other hand out to him, but he didn't see it. After a minute, she pulled it back.

"It's my turn for a question," Mom said, still looking at Chuck. "What did you two talk about at the cemetery after your daddy's funeral?" She turned her gaze on Lori. "When no one but Chuck could convince you it was time to go home?"

Lori looked puzzled.

"I don't remember that," she said. "I remember seeing the coffin, at the funeral home, and everybody saying Daddy was inside. I remember Gram feeding me cherry Life Savers during the service, so I'd be quiet. I haven't eaten them since. I don't remember the cemetery."

Chuck looked down, studying the whorls in the table's wood. They circled back on themselves endlessly. He couldn't believe Lori had forgotten. Was she just being polite? Was she keeping secrets for him, the way she used to?

It didn't matter. Chuck had to confess.

"I told Lori—" He made himself say it. "I told her that Daddy wanted her to go home. That he was waiting for us there."

Familiar guilt swept over him. He could remember exactly how he'd felt, standing beside Lori in the cemetery, a little boy sent to do what grown-ups couldn't accomplish. He could almost feel the thin cotton of his church pants blowing against his bony legs. He'd wanted to cry, like Lori was doing, but Pop had told him boys weren't allowed. Then Lori had looked at him with big, trusting eyes, and he'd said the first thing that popped into his mind.

"I lied," he said now. "I knew it was a lie. But I wanted to believe it, too. I thought if I said that, maybe it would be true."

Lori gasped.

"I remember now!" she said. "Then we went home, and Daddy wasn't there, and I was so mad at you. You kept saying, 'Just wait. Just wait. He's coming.' And I kept waiting. I'd sit by the front window every day, watching for him. You promised me! I thought it was all your fault that he didn't come. And then I forgot I was even waiting for Daddy, but I was still mad at you."

Chuck nodded, barely hearing her words, except for "mad at you."

"Yes," he whispered. "I—I don't blame you. You should have been mad at me."

He looked up, and Mom was staring at them both, her face flooded with dismay.

"Oh, no," she said. "I'm so sorry. I didn't know—Chuck, it wasn't your fault. It wasn't your fault, either, Lori. I just—someone gave me a book about how kids deal with grief, but I never had time to read it. If only . . ."

Chuck stared back blankly. Lori shrugged.

"What good would that have done?" she asked. "Neither of us told you what was wrong. We were just being stupid. We just didn't want to believe that Daddy was never coming back." She looked across the table at Chuck. "I shouldn't have been mad at you," she said. "I'm not mad at you anymore. It's over. It's all in the past."

Saying that, Lori realized it was true. The place where all her fury lived was gone. The walls had broken down, and it had all washed away.

Chuck closed his eyes, waiting for some sense of relief. Lori forgave him. She wasn't mad anymore. Why didn't he feel good? He opened his eyes, still bothered, still worried. Still guilty.

Mom reached down and gathered up the travel brochures and guidebooks.

"Anybody in the mood for Disneyland now?" she asked. "We really ought to get out of the hotel room."

Lori grimaced.

"I don't feel like Disneyland," she said. "Or Hollywood. But does—does Los Angeles have an art museum?"

"I think so," Mom said.

She and Lori both turned and looked at Chuck, questioningly. He kept staring down at the table, listening to an argument in his head. *Tell! No, no, I can't. But this might be your only chance.*

He opened his mouth.

"I was drawing when they came in to tell me Daddy died," he began slowly. "I wasn't supposed to be. I was supposed to be doing math. Mrs. Swain warned me, lots of times, that I'd get in trouble if I drew instead of paying attention. Then Daddy died. I thought—"

"You thought it was your fault?" Lori asked incredulously.

Chuck nodded slowly.

"I decided I'd never draw again," he said. "And I didn't. Even when I wanted to. Even when I was flunking art."

"You flunked art?" Lori asked in disbelief.

"And I didn't notice," Mom muttered, almost as if she were talking to herself. "That was the one F I didn't think to worry about."

Chuck didn't seem to hear his sister or his mother.

"Then on this trip, away from home . . . it seemed like maybe it'd be okay to draw again." Chuck's words came so slowly, it was excruciating. "To go to art museums and all. Like I was free. For-forgiven. And then in Phoenix—what happened there—it started to seem wrong again. . . ."

Mom laid her hand on Chuck's arm.

"Oh, Chuck," she murmured. "I—" She hesitated, as if searching for the most comforting words. Lori wasn't so cautious.

"You really thought Daddy died because you were drawing instead of doing math?" she asked. "And you quit drawing because of that? Are you crazy?"

"Lori!" Mom exclaimed.

But Chuck didn't scurry back into his usual shell. He looked up slowly.

"It is crazy, isn't it?" he asked.

"You were thinking like a seven-year-old," Mom said. "That's all. And because nobody tried hard enough to find out what was wrong, you never escaped the guilt. Or the guilt about what you told Lori. It's my fault. I'm sorry. I'm so sorry."

Her voice was so full of pain that Lori and Chuck both reached for her at the same time.

"It's okay," Lori said. "Really."

"Yeah," Chuck echoed. "It's okay. Now."

Chuck

Lori and Mom let Chuck have the window seat for the flight home.

"You like looking at things more than I do," Lori said.

Chuck started to protest, then he realized she didn't mean it as an insult. It was a flat statement of fact. He did like looking at things more than Lori did. He slipped into the row of seats, put his backpack on the floor, buckled the seat belt.

The flight attendant down the aisle launched into the safety lecture, but Chuck didn't listen. He closed his eyes instead, visualizing his favorite pictures from the art museum the day before. If he remembered them well enough, he could look at them anytime he wanted for the rest of his life—sitting in algebra class, plowing a field, pressure-spraying the hog barn. He couldn't believe Lori had asked to go to the art museum.

She did that for you, a little voice whispered in his head.

And she hadn't done it to mock him. She'd stood behind him, gazing at the paintings with him, as if she'd honestly wanted to understand.

This was going to take some getting used to, Lori being nice to him again.

"Ready to go home?" Mom asked beside him now.

"I guess," Chuck said, his mind still back on Lori and the museum.

"You don't feel sick, do you?" Mom asked.

Chuck shook his head and held up his wrists to show his airsickness bracelets. They were taking off, and he hadn't even noticed. He wasn't scared at all now. What was the big deal? People flew all the time.

The plane's engine roared beneath his feet, sounding ever so slightly like a tractor engine. For the first time, Chuck felt a pang of homesickness. How could he be thinking of tractors longingly?

They left the city behind, far below, and flew out over mountains—mountains and desert, landscapes so foreign to Chuck that they seemed to belong to a different planet. There'd been mountain and desert paintings at the museum yesterday. Chuck closed his eyes again, but this time what he pictured against his eyelids was the pattern of sunlight on corn leaves, of soybean rows flowing toward the horizon, of wheat stalks bowing in the wind.

He hadn't seen any of those designs in any of the museums he'd visited. Someone needed to draw those or paint those or sculpt those—or something.

No, he thought. *I need to.*

Without thinking, Chuck turned to his mother.

"Remember what you offered?" he asked. "Can I still—I mean, will you still pay for art lessons?"

Mom looked up. Smiled.

"Of course," she said. "Absolutely."

Chuck felt a shot of joy. For just a second, he felt the usual guilt: *Drawing is bad. Daddy died because I was drawing.* But then the guilt was gone. He could draw, and it was okay.

They were in clouds now, high above the earth. The pilot announced he was turning off the seat belts sign. Chuck stared out the window, losing himself in following the arcs of cloud against the wings of the plane. Such designs. He wanted to draw those, too. He didn't have another notebook yet, but maybe when he got home . . .

When he got home, there'd be chores. Two weeks' worth, if he knew Pop. And then Mike and Joey would probably make fun of him if he tried drawing anywhere around them. And at school, his drawing would just be something else for the other kids to laugh at. Or destroy.

"Ready to go home?" Mom had asked him. And he'd said he was. Why? He felt a weight settle on his shoulders. He felt like an escaped criminal who'd been caught, getting sent back to prison. He might as well be wearing handcuffs. What if the trip hadn't changed anything?

But it had.

187

Chuck remembered when one of their neighbors had died, trapped in a corn bin the year before. He'd gotten buried in corn and suffocated. Chuck could remember Pop describing the accident to Gram: "He just didn't have any room to breathe," Pop had said, again and again, shaking his head. It was like Pop had to repeat the words to make himself understand.

And Chuck had lain awake nights picturing the man, kernels of corn packed against his eyes and ears and face and nose, with no room to breathe. *That's me,* Chuck had thought. *I'm suffocating, too.* He was surrounded by what Pop wanted and what the kids at school said about him and what the teachers said about him and what his own brothers and sisters thought about him. And what he thought about himself.

But now—Lori had given him some space, and Mom had given him some space, and the pictures he carried around in his head would give him some space, and art lessons would give him some space. And what space he didn't have, he'd make.

Nobody can suffocate me now, Chuck thought, and it was a surprise. A happy one.

Lori

They were in the sky for the last time. The flight attendants had brought out a meal and cleared it away. Just about everyone else seemed to be sleeping now, heads bobbing uncomfortably on pillows no bigger than lunch bags.

Lori was too antsy for sleep. She flicked through her magazine—*Seventeen*, again—but it couldn't hold her interest. Down the row, Chuck was peering eagerly out the window, and Mom was scribbling notes to prepare for yet another speech. Mom caught Lori's eyes on her and made a face.

"If I do this now, I won't have to worry about it once we get home," she said. "I'll have four whole days off before I leave for Kalamazoo."

"Don't tell Gram," Lori said. "She'll put you to work scrubbing windows and shelling peas."

Mom laughed and went back to writing.

Lori regarded her mother through half-closed eyes. *Poor Mom,* she thought, surprising herself. *"Poor Mom"? "Poor Mom"? All those fancy hotels and expensive meals and applause every night, and I'm thinking, "Poor Mom"?* But fancy hotels were just empty rooms in strange cities, and the applause was just a bunch of strangers hitting their hands together.

Lori remembered how she'd thought of Mom as the Ancient Mariner, and it was true; Mom was just as trapped, her speeches were just as much an albatross around her neck. Mom kept saying the same thing over and over and over again, and she couldn't stop any more than the Ancient Mariner could.

"When you're on the twenty-ninth minute of your half-hour speech . . ." "When you're down to the last second in your time-bank account . . ." "When you're signing the last line on the contract of life . . ."

Before she had time to change her mind, Lori leaned over and tapped her mother on the arm.

"You and Daddy had a fight, didn't you?" she asked. "The day he died."

Mom looked startled. She stared at Lori for a long time, and Lori felt like Mom was judging her, just as she had two weeks earlier, on the first flight. But this time Lori knew that Mom wasn't going to push her away or shut her out. Lori didn't have to worry about being found unworthy. Very slowly, Mom began to nod.

"Yes," she said, drawing the word out, like a whisper,

an echo, a memory. "Oh, Lori, we were both so tired. And Mikey was getting into everything, and Joey was teething and crying all the time. . . . Those aren't excuses, just . . . reasons. Tom didn't take the time to kiss me good-bye when he walked out that door, and I yelled at him about it. And he yelled back. . . . It was just a stupid little spat. Nothing I would have remembered even a day later if—if only . . ."

Mom didn't have to finish the sentence.

Lori felt like Mom had just handed her the last piece of a complicated puzzle. No, she corrected herself—probably not the last piece. But the last piece that Lori needed to see the picture clearly. To understand.

"That's why you keep telling me not to get married too young," Lori said. "So I don't have a stupid fight with my husband someday and have him die without either one of us apologizing."

Mom frowned at Lori doubtfully.

"But what do I know, anyway?" she said. "People always have stupid fights."

Mom and I are really talking, Lori marveled. *We can do that now.* She and Mom probably had more stupid fights ahead, themselves. But Lori would never again feel like she'd felt in Chicago, when Mom was hiding everything and Lori was lashing out, desperate to learn anything. She'd never again feel like she'd felt the whole past year, when she couldn't even look at Mom without wanting to scream.

Lori glanced up, and the FASTEN SEAT BELTS sign had blinked

on again. The pilot came on the P.A. system to announce that they were about to land. Mom went back to her speech.

So we can talk in midair, thirty thousand feet above the ground, Lori thought. *Will we still be able to talk after we get home?*

Lori wanted to think so. But it was hard to think at all, with so much jumping around in her mind. She stared at the seat in front of her, but her eyes saw a potted tree in a fancy hotel, a street full of dark faces, her brother's drawings. Over the hum of the plane's engine, her ears still heard her mother's voice on tape: "By the grace of God, we'll get by." How could Lori go home, knowing what she knew now? How could home still be home, if Lori was different?

The plane angled downward. Lori welcomed the pressure in her ears. She thought about leaning over and telling Mom, *You know, I really did think we were going to crash when we were landing in Los Angeles.* Then she and Mom could laugh about that together.

But they were already on the ground. The wheels hissed on wet pavement, seeming to say, *Almost there, almost there.* Almost home. This was the landing Lori had been longing for the entire trip. But it didn't bring the relief she'd expected. It didn't feel right.

Lori gulped and picked up her backpack, still feeling jangly and strange. She held it on her knees, waiting.

The plane pulled up to the gate and stopped. People stood up all around her, like puppets on invisible strings.

Lori waited while businesspeople pulled rolling luggage down the aisle, while grandmothers tugged shopping bags behind them. When she couldn't stand it any longer, Lori lunged out in front of a guy with a shaved head and a ring in his nose.

What's he doing in Ohio? Lori wondered. She imagined him wandering around Pickford County peering at everyone with the same bafflement Lori had had looking at people in L.A. She giggled, and the guy actually smiled at her, companionably, as if they had something in common.

Maybe they did.

In the ramp leading to the airport, Lori stopped and waited for Mom and Chuck, who hadn't crowded in front of anyone. So the three of them stepped through the door together, and were practically knocked down by a human torpedo.

"Mom! Lori! Chuck!" It was Emma, trying to wrap her arms around all three of them at once. Lori saw Gram and Mike and Joey waiting right behind her.

"I missed you!" Emma shrieked.

Gram had fixed Emma's blond hair in a single ponytail, practically on the very top of her head. She looked like a Kewpie doll. Lori felt an unbelievable rush of love for Emma, who wasn't even born when Daddy died, who didn't remember a time when Mommy didn't travel. Lori threw her arms around Emma and lifted her off the ground, spun her around.

"Missed you, too," she whispered.

"What a nice surprise," Mom was saying to Gram. "You didn't have to—"

Gram waved Mom's concerns away.

"Oh, I knew you had the car, and I know I should be home weeding the garden—wait till you see how much it's grown—but we just couldn't wait another hour. Could we, Emma?"

Emma shook her head so hard, the end of her ponytail whipped from side to side. She slid her hand into Mom's and said, "I had to tell you about my piano recital. I played 'Frère Jacques' without making a single mistake, and everyone clapped, and Pop said I was the best eight-year-old in the whole show—"

"Dummy. You were the *only* eight-year-old in the whole show," Mike jeered.

"And all of the seven-year-olds were better than you," Joey added.

Lori regarded her younger brothers seriously.

What if you knew what I knew? she wondered. *What if Mom told you what happened when Daddy died? Would you feel like making fun of other people then?* But they didn't know what Lori knew, and Lori was glad. She wanted to protect them. And because she didn't know what else to do, she got Joey in a headlock and rubbed his hair with her knuckles and said, "Good to see you're as big a brat as ever." Mike moved out of range before she could reach him, but he stuck his tongue out at her, and she stuck out hers right back.

"So was 'Frère Jacques' the only song you played, or

did you do that other one, too? What's it called?" Mom was asking Emma.

"'Country Gardens,' Mom," Emma said, looking up trustingly.

"She just did the one," Gram interrupted. "They had twenty kids playing—one song per kid was plenty."

Out of habit, Lori started to glare at her mother, thinking, *If you'd been there, you'd know. What kind of mother misses her own daughter's piano recital?* But as Mom turned to straighten the straps on Emma's jumper, Lori caught sight of the glitter of pain in her mother's eyes. She remembered what Mom had said, only the day before: "You all could be kids who got free lunches at school and bought all your clothes from yard sales; or I could go on the road, and you could have piano lessons and dance lessons and pay 4-H club dues and wear the same clothes as everyone else." Did Mom think it was worth it? Did Lori?

For once, Lori didn't know. She was just glad she hadn't had to make the decision Mom had faced.

Everyone began walking toward the baggage claim area. Lori's family was a rowdy group, with Joey and Mike playfully punching each other and Emma skipping on the colored squares of the floor. Gram pulled Lori and Chuck close and began quizzing them.

"You just didn't send enough postcards!" she scolded. "What was the weather like? What was your favorite city?"

Lori and Chuck exchanged glances. It was like what

they'd done as little kids, conferring without words: *Do you suppose they know we pulled all the green apples off the tree? I won't say anything if you don't say anything. . . . Will they get madder that we left the gate open if we don't tell them the pigs are out in the garden, eating all the peas?* Lori had missed that camaraderie, that sense of conspiracy, more than she'd even realized. It was like having an arm or leg amputated, years before, and suddenly getting it back.

She thought back to the Los Angeles art museum the day before. It'd been boring. That was what she wanted to think. But every now and then, standing with Chuck before some painting, she'd squinted hard and almost understood.

He was going to be a great artist. She just knew it. And she was going to make sure everyone else knew it, too.

But for now, she said only what Chuck's eyes told her to say.

"Everyplace was nice," Lori said politely. "And the weather was great."

Lori *liked* Gram. There was a part of her that wanted to tell Gram at least some of what had really happened on the trip. But it was too hard.

This is what it's like to be Mom, Lori thought. *To carry around secrets you can't speak of.*

In Lori's mind's eye, she saw a ball of fire, a tractor burning, and Mom watching in horror, a stupid argument still echoing in her ears. It should be worse for Lori to have that image in her head, that secret in her care. But it wasn't.

She knew her mother now.

Gram began chattering about the fair queen nominees being announced and the tomato bugs infesting the other end of the county. Lori glanced at the posters on the walls they were passing. She was surprised that they looked so familiar: A beautiful woman and a gorgeous man lay in sand under the words CLUB MED. Above them, a jet took off into an incredible sunrise. Suddenly Lori realized why she recognized them. She'd passed the same posters two weeks ago, on her way to Chicago. In fact, she and Mom and Chuck had sat in the waiting area right on the other side of the hall.

Lori had a sudden, strange feeling that all she had to do was turn her head and she'd see a girl in a homemade sundress in the second seat from the right, squirming in embarrassment, waiting for her first plane trip. How long ago that seemed, when Lori actually thought that what she wore mattered most. Lori didn't even know where the sundress was now—wadded up in the bottom of her suitcase, probably. Or left behind, forgotten, in some hotel room. You lost things, traveling.

And found things.

". . . the new extension agent—Bud Pike, you know, that really nice guy?—he had a whole column in the paper yesterday on tips for getting rid of the tomato bugs. I sent the kids out, looking for them, but they couldn't find a single one in our garden," Gram was saying.

Lori threw her arms around her grandmother and said, "I love you, Gram."

Gram gave her a startled look and straightened her dress.

"Well, you, too, I'm sure," she said, and went on talking about tomato bugs.

They took the escalator down to the baggage claim, pulled their luggage off the conveyor belts.

"Don't you wish there was a bellhop or a taxi driver nearby?" Lori teased Chuck as he heaved yet another stuffed suitcase to the ground.

He looked at her very seriously.

"No," he said. "That never once felt right, letting someone else carry my bags." He peered off into the distance, past Lori. "You know, if I ever go anywhere again, I'm not going to let them."

"Oh," Lori said. She watched him skillfully hoist the suitcases onto a cart. Had he gotten taller on this trip, or was he just standing up straight for once? She remembered how he hadn't even bothered to open the peanut packs the flight attendants had given him on the plane, how he'd turned down the chance to eat the rest of Mom's lunch. What had happened to the brother she'd left home with?

She knew. She just didn't fully understand.

Luggage in tow, they all headed out to Mom's car and Gram's truck. Lori and Chuck went with Gram, and the other kids went with Mom.

"Guess Mom's had enough of us after two weeks," Lori joked as they pulled out of the parking garage.

"Don't think so. It kills her leaving you. You know that, don't you?" Gram said.

Oh, yeah. That's why she keeps leaving, Lori started to say, out of habit. Then the words registered for once.

Gram has been telling me that for years, Lori realized with a shock. *But I never heard her before.*

"Yeah," Lori said quietly. "I know."

Gram stopped in the middle of fumbling in her purse for money to pay the parking attendant. She gave Lori a startled look.

"Good," she said softly.

Soon they were out on the interstate, Gram muttering under her breath about the city traffic.

"Now, why would anyone want to live in a place like this?" she asked.

"The people here probably say the same thing about Pickford County," Chuck said.

Gram laughed.

"Fair enough," she said. "I'm just as glad all of them *don't* want to live there."

Lori felt muddled. Chuck was different. She was different. Mom was different. How could everything else stay the same? Lori tried to ignore her growing sense of dread. She leaned forward in the seat, as if that would get her home to Pickford County faster.

After miles of stop-and-start traffic, they left the city

and its gridlock behind. Out in the country, they zoomed past fields of corn and beans and golden winter wheat, ready for harvest.

I haven't seen a cornfield in two weeks, Lori realized with a jolt. She drank in the sight. In the two weeks she'd been away, the corn had grown from knee high to waist high. It was like coming back to find toddlers transformed into teenagers. *I missed it all,* Lori thought. But it was silly to feel sad about corn.

Gram pulled off on the Pickford County exit, and soon they were traveling down achingly familiar roads. Lori stared joyously at sights she'd never thought about missing: the old corncrib rusting behind the Brownleys' barn, the Riptons' metal mailbox leaning toward the road, the tiger lilies growing wild in the ditch. She had missed them. Unbearably.

Then they were turning into their own lane. Swaying above the porch, Gram's hanging flower baskets were full of blooms now, instead of mere buds. The morning glories had climbed higher on the lamppost. One of the tabby kittens tumbled down the porch steps, and he was bigger than two weeks ago, almost full grown.

Lori felt like she was seeing everything with two sets of eyes or thinking with two separate brains. Part of her was still the pretrip Lori, and part of her was—she didn't know who she was now. It was like she didn't recognize her own home anymore. Had the shutters always been such a bright shade of green? Had the weeping willow in the front yard always been such a huge tree? Everything looked different than she remembered. And, somehow, at the same time, everything was so familiar, she felt like she'd never left.

That's what Mom meant, Lori thought, *when she said she would never leave Pickford County.*

Lori hadn't left, either. She'd just carried Pickford County around with her, everywhere she went. She understood now how that worked. She could fly to the moon and not lose Pickford County. And not lose herself.

It's ground into our souls. Like dirt, Lori thought.

That was such a silly thing to think that she laughed out loud.

"Glad to be home?" Gram asked.

Lori looked out the window again. Somehow her two ways of seeing merged into one. She couldn't separate out her reactions anymore. She just saw.

"Yeah," she answered Gram. "We all are."